A WHOLE NEW WORLD

Marla's attempts to become an actress and model have stalled. While she decides what to do next, she goes to live in her dead uncle's house in the country, with its tantalising clues to his mysterious past. Then comes an unexpected chance to restart her modelling career — but if she seizes this opportunity it will mean abandoning the new life she has made for herself, and not only new friends but also a possible romance. Which should she choose?

SHEILA HOLROYD

---◆---

A WHOLE
NEW WORLD

Complete and Unabridged

LINFORD
Leicester

First published in Great Britain in 2013

First Linford Edition
published 2015

*A catalogue record for this book is available
from the British Library.*

ISBN 978–1–4448–2479–7

Published by
F. A. Thorpe (Publishing)

1

'And, as you can see, the instrument panel is very well designed,' Marla said brightly.

The man who claimed to be interested in the car she was demonstrating nodded wisely and edged even nearer to her. She looked round desperately, but though the motor show was crowded no one else was waiting to ask her questions and Bill Able, who was in charge of the stand for this latest model of a family saloon, was busy taking down the details of a couple who seemed genuinely interested in buying. Marla cursed the publicity agents who had decided that pretty girls in skin-tight mini-dresses would attract car buyers. Admittedly it gave her a job, but there were always some men who used the excuse of looking at the car as an opportunity to get close to the girls and examine them in detail rather than the car.

'Where's the switch for the radio?' asked the middle-aged man, grinning at her and not even pretending to look at the car.

'There.' She pointed.

'Where?'

She leant inside the car and put her finger on the button.

'Oh, I see.'

He had put his hand on her back as he finally bent down to look, and suddenly she felt his hand slide down and momentarily clasp her buttock. She sprang up, hitting her head on the window frame, swung round, and slapped him hard across his face. He yelped.

Moments before, the rest of the motor show had seemed oblivious of her existence, but now every head seemed to turn in her direction and there was a sudden hush. She heard Bill Able's voice raised in horror.

'Marla, what are you doing?'

'Resigning!' she snapped, tearing off the sash she wore emblazoned with the name of the car firm. She let it drop to the floor at the feet of the offender, who stood with a hand clasped to his face. She strode away from the stand, only to be confronted by an indignant woman.

'That's my husband you hit!' she was informed.

'You have my sympathy,' Marla said crisply, and walked on. She looked back briefly when she reached the exit and saw the woman standing in front of her husband, her hands on her hips. He was obviously going to have difficulty explaining what had provoked the slap.

Marla went to the changing room, wriggled out of the mini-dress and put on her usual jeans and sweater, collected her few belongings from her locker and walked out of the building, her head held high. She had hit the man so hard that her palm was still stinging, and she was glad. She was tired of sweaty, over-familiar men; tired of trying to avoid their alcohol-scented breath, and the slap had been a satisfying revenge. She caught a bus into town and, back in the shelter of her temporary bed-sit, she made herself a cup of coffee and sank down into a battered armchair.

It was not meant to be like this. She had left school confident that a career as a successful actress lay before her, but the years since then had taught her that a pretty face and an ability to memorise lines was not enough. She lacked the spark that could bring a character to life, and although her dark-haired good looks had brought her a few appearances in provincial theatres, she had had to earn enough to live on by modelling, usually for catalogues, and taking temporary jobs like the one at the motor show.

Now what was she going to do? Word would soon spread among the agencies about the slap, and although they might understand the provocation and sympathise, they would be reluctant to hire someone who might inflict actual bodily harm on potential customers. She wondered how Bill Able had dealt with the situation. They got on well with each other and had been out together for a couple of pleasant evenings, and she regretted having put him in an awkward position.

At that moment there was a knock on the door and Marla opened it to find her landlady, Mrs Strange, standing there, smiling a little anxiously.

'Hello, Miss Merton. I heard you come in so I thought I'd pop up and collect the rent.'

'Of course. Just a moment.' Marla opened her handbag, found her purse, and counted out the money. There was not much left in the purse when she had given Mrs Strange the rent.

The landlady thanked her but still hovered in the doorway. 'I noticed you were home early today,' she said brightly. 'Nothing wrong, is there? I thought the motor show stayed open for a few hours yet.'

'It does, but my boss said I could have a few hours off,' Marla said, and shut the door.

Mrs Strange was clearly anxious to make sure that Marla was still gainfully employed and could therefore pay for her accommodation. After all, Marla had originally rented the bed-sit with another girl, Thelma, which had made the rent affordable, but three weeks earlier Thelma had been offered a better job in another part of the country and Marla was finding it a struggle to pay for the bed-sit from just what she earned. She had a vision of herself out of work and homeless, wandering the streets, and she sniffed dolefully. But just as she was preparing to spend a little time wallowing in self-pity, there was a sharp tap on the door. She opened it, wondering whether it was Mrs Strange again, but to her relief she saw Bill Able.

'Come in!' she exclaimed eagerly, holding the door wide. 'I hoped you'd have a chance to come to see me. I could do with a little comforting and I think I could do with some career advice as well.'

She stopped. Instead of coming in and taking her in his arms for a friendly hug, Bill Able stood apart from her, his face grim. 'Comfort you?' he said incredulously. 'After the scene you made? I thought the whole stand was going to be closed down. I had to spend ages calming down the man and his wife and then someone got on to the manufacturer's publicity department, and I've had to deal with them as well as the show's organisers. You created havoc and then walked out and left me in an impossible situation.'

'But that awful man was groping me!'

'So what? You know perfectly well that it happens all the time. If you didn't want that kind of nuisance you shouldn't have taken the job.'

She gasped. 'So I should have just smiled and let him carry on?'

He shrugged. 'What harm would it have done? You know what to expect. You're standing there in a short, tight dress, smiling away. Some men see it as an open invitation to get familiar, but you're supposed to be able to deal with it quietly. You're there to help sell cars

7

to them, not hit them in the face!'

Marla turned away from him. 'Get out! I don't care what you've come to say; I'm not going back to the show.'

'Of course you're not. You're sacked.' He took an envelope from his pocket and tossed it on the table. 'There's the documentation and the money you're owed. Goodbye.' He strode off without a backward glance.

Marla sat down and, to her own annoyance, burst into tears, but she was soon wiping her eyes and scolding herself for being so silly. She opened the envelope, added its contents to those of her purse, and decided that she had to find more work as soon as possible. She had to forget what had happened and be purposeful about the future.

A quick trip to a nearby corner shop gave her a copy of the local newspaper and she spread it out on the floor and got out a pen, ready to mark possible jobs in 'Situations Vacant'. The result was disappointing, as most of the advertisements required specific skills which she lacked. Office work was out, as she had never learned to type or mastered the computer. Besides, she wanted a job she could give up at short notice if work as a model or actress was offered her.

She rang a few numbers who had offered work in restaurants or pubs, but the paper had come out some days before and all the positions were filled. That left just one advertisement. It was for work in a club and Marla lingered reluctantly over this. Still, she had done the occasional stint in bars, and though the club's opening hours from late evening to early morning were definitely unattractive, beggars couldn't be choosers. She called the number given and was asked a few questions, such as her age and previous experience. When she said she had worked as an actress and a model the bored voice at the other end began to show interest and she was asked to come for an interview. She was used to this reaction. Everybody expected glamour from an actress.

When she found the address the next afternoon she hesitated before ringing the bell. The black-painted door was scuffed and shabby, though possibly it might look better at night when the neon lights above it were lit. An unshaven man in a creased shirt who was badly in need of a shower yawned as he led her across a stale-smelling dance floor in semi-darkness to the manager's office where her guide knocked, opened the door, said, 'She's here,' and abandoned her.

The middle-aged man did not rise as she came in. Instead he just nodded and pointed at a chair in front of his desk. He stared across at her, inspecting her inch by inch, and Marla, uncomfortably conscious of his gaze resting on her legs, tried to pull down her skirt.

'You've worked in clubs before, Miss Merton?'

'Not in clubs, but I've worked in bars and hotels.'

'What did you do?'

'I've been a barmaid, a waitress,

worked in reception . . . '

He nodded, cutting her off. 'So you're used to being nice to the customers?'

'Yes, of course.' She felt a stab of guilt as she thought of the man she had slapped. That was one customer she had not been nice to!

He leant back. 'Well, this job involves bar work and other duties, but the most important thing for our hostesses is to be nice to the customers — very nice, if you get my meaning.' He looked her over again. 'If a customer wants to dance with you, you dance with him. If he wants you to sit and have a few drinks with him, then that's what you do. You keep the customer happy. You can make quite a bit of money on the side if you want to. Do you understand?'

The meaning was becoming far too clear. Marla knew that no matter how desperate she was for money she was not going to work here, 'being very nice to the customers'.

She pushed back her chair and stood up. 'I'm sorry,' she said, 'but I've made a mistake. I serve drinks, that's all. Goodbye.'

He slapped his hands on his desk and stood up, glaring at her, and she fled from the room and across the dance floor, through the shabby door and almost ran along the street.

Back in her room she was too agitated to sit, and paced the floor. What was she going to do now? She could stay where she was for a few days, but after that, unless she could get more money she would be unable to pay the rent. She looked round. Her work took her all over the country and she had no home base, living in a succession of lodgings. Mrs Strange's bed-sit was typical. The room was quietly shabby, the carpet worn and the thin curtains barely keeping out the light, but it was her refuge from the rest of the world, somewhere to rest and recuperate.

'Don't be stupid. You'll find something. You always have before,' she told herself, and then just as she was blowing her nose yet again her mobile phone rang. She picked it up fearfully, wondering who it was, but a male voice greeted her cheerfully.

'Hello, pet!'

It was her father. He and her mother had retired to a small house in Spain two years earlier, and were enjoying themselves thoroughly. Phone calls from them were infrequent, so was this more trouble?

'Dad! How are you? And Mother?'

'We're both fine. You must come and see us again soon. How are you? Still waiting for your big break?' Before she could answer he went on. 'Actually, I'm calling because we need a little help. You've heard me speak of Uncle Andrew, my father's brother?'

'I've heard you mention him once or twice, though I've never met him.'

'He was a lot younger than my father and I only met him once when I was still a child, and he disappeared about twelve years ago. Anyway, I'm afraid

13

you won't get the opportunity to meet him now because he died about a month ago, and I've just heard from his solicitor that he's left everything to me.'

Marla squeaked.

'Don't get excited,' her father cautioned. 'I think I'm his heir because he couldn't think of anyone else. After all, we haven't had any direct contact since that one meeting. And he hasn't left much. As far as I can make out, there's a little house in Cheshire and its contents in some town called Woodham, and that's all.' His voice grew wheedling. 'Now, your mother and I don't want to have to fly back to England and spend weeks sorting things out. It could cost as much as the estate is worth. But I thought, if you had a gap between jobs, perhaps you could pop up to Cheshire, see the solicitor, clear out the cottage and arrange for it to be sold. Of course, we'd pay you something for your time out of the proceeds.'

Marla was thinking quickly. This could get her out of London till the slap had been forgotten.

'You mean there's an empty furnished house waiting in Cheshire? Could I live in it while I sorted it all out?'

'I don't see why not. Will you do it?'

'I'd be delighted to help. Actually I'm free just now so it would be quite convenient. Give me the solicitor's address.' She scribbled it down as her father dictated it and told him when she could go.

'I'll contact him and say you have the authority to do whatever is necessary,' he said. 'Bless you, my child.'

Mrs Strange did not seem surprised when Marla said she wanted to leave in a couple of days. She had probably been listening to the confrontation with Bill Able.

'A double room is expensive for one person,' she said resignedly, 'especially if you haven't got a steady job . . . ' She eyed Marla. 'Of course, you are supposed to give a week's notice and pay the full rent even if you're not staying that long.'

Marla's lips tightened and she decided to call the landlady's bluff. 'Well, I haven't actually got to rush off, so if I've got to pay the rent anyway I might as well stay . . . '

'No need for that,' Mrs Strange said hastily. 'Lucky for you, I have had an enquiry from two sisters who are looking for a room and I did tell them that I might have something suitable soon. If they want to move in quickly I can probably let you off a few pounds.'

Fortunately the sisters were eager to move in as soon as possible, so Marla managed to argue herself out of paying any more rent, and in a couple of days a combination of coaches and buses delivered Marla at the small Cheshire town of Woodham.

The journey had been the cheapest method of transport available, but had involved changes at coach stations which rang with noise and never had enough seats, and it had been very tiring. As the coach drew away she stood forlornly on the pavement, virtually all her worldly goods in two suitcases at her feet. It was late afternoon and gloomy with the threat of rain hanging in the air, reminding her that winter was coming and it would be Christmas before long.

She looked round at the small shops lining the street. Now she had to find the solicitor's office, and then somehow get herself to her great-uncle's house after claiming the key. She wondered whether she could do that in a couple of hours before daylight faded completely. Perhaps she should try to find somewhere in the town to stay for the night? But a hotel would cost money she couldn't afford, so she sighed and gripped the handles of her cases, preparing to drag them through the streets till she found the solicitor. After all, if this was the main street it shouldn't take very long.

'Excuse me.'

She turned. A tall, fair-haired young man in a grey suit was smiling down at her. She frowned impatiently. She really did not want someone trying to pick her up now.

'Yes?' she said as coldly as she could.

'Are you Miss Merton — Miss Marla Merton?' She nodded, and his smile grew wider. 'My name's John Ericson. I am one of the solicitors handling your great-uncle's estate. Your father contacted us and said you would be arriving today by coach and I calculated that you would probably be here about this time, so I came to show you the way to our office.' He stepped forward and took the cases from her. 'It's only five minutes' walk.'

Without waiting for her response he set off with the cases, and Marla had no choice but to follow him. His stride lengthened and she had to hurry to keep up with him. Then she stopped dead as she realised he had not given her any proof of his identity. Perhaps he was just a petty thief trying to steal her cases! But then he would not have known her name or where she was going, so she hurried to catch up and continued to follow the young man grimly, noticing that he did not look round once to check what she was doing and slightly annoyed that he had taken her agreement for granted. But at least his appearance meant that one problem was solved, as she no longer had to worry about hunting for his office.

Soon they reached a black-and-white building which announced discreetly that it belonged to George Ericson and Son, Solicitors, and he was ushering her into a neat office where a receptionist looked up from her computer as they entered. 'Tea for two in my office, please, Beryl,' requested John Ericson. 'And a few biscuits if you can find them.'

He took Marla on into a room dominated by a large mahogany desk, indicated that she should sit in the comfortable leather chair in front of it, put the cases down in a corner, and then took his own seat behind the desk and leant back, frowning slightly.

'As a formality, have you any proof of your identity?' She had expected this and showed him her passport, which he inspected and returned. 'Your father has emailed us giving you full authority to deal with all matters relating to your great-uncle's estate, but he didn't give any details about exactly what you intended to do when you got here.' His tone implied that he deplored this lack of efficiency.

'That's because I don't know myself yet,' Marla said defensively. 'I don't know what there is, what it's worth, and what should be done with it or how long the process will take. I know you sent some details to my father, but he hasn't passed much on to me.'

'I see,' John Ericson said thoughtfully, his lips pursing with the disapproval he did not voice. Marla decided she hadn't got the energy at that time to defend her father's rather haphazard approach to business.

At that moment the door opened and the receptionist, Beryl, appeared with a large tea tray. John Ericson pushed aside a few documents and cleared a space for it on the desk. Beryl, a trim blonde in her mid-forties, smiled at him. 'I managed to find your favourite biscuits,' she told him.

'Thank you,' he replied, as if he had expected no less.

Beryl smiled at him again and then left the room after giving Marla a long look, as though assessing her suitability as a client. John Ericson prepared to pour out the tea.

'Milk in the cup first or afterwards?' he enquired.

'Afterwards,' Marla chose. She usually put a teabag in a mug, added hot water and stirred, so she found the ritual with the delicate china quite unnecessary and time-wasting. She took the cup of tea gratefully, however, realising that this was the first hot drink she'd had since she left London. She drank it thirstily and accepted the offer of a refill which she drank more slowly, warming her cold hands on the cup.

She knew the young solicitor was inspecting her and was unpleasantly aware of the poor impression her rather bedraggled appearance must have been making.

The tea drunk, the biscuits eaten, they turned back to business. 'Essentially Mr Merton's estate consists of the house and its contents,' the young solicitor explained. 'The money in his bank account is enough to pay outstanding bills, but there is not much left. What there is will be paid into the bank account you nominate.'

'How soon?' Marla interrupted. She needed that money as soon as possible.

'I can't say. Probably just a few weeks.' Not the answer she had hoped for.

He hesitated then, glancing at his watch and then out of the window at the gathering darkness. 'It is getting late, Miss Merton, and you must be tired after your journey.' His look made her aware again of her exhausted, rather untidy appearance. 'Perhaps you'd prefer to continue this discussion tomorrow. Have you booked into a hotel? If so, I can drive you there. If not, let me find you a room.' He stretched out a hand towards his telephone, but Marla shook her head quickly.

'I don't want a hotel, thank you. I thought I could stay in my great-uncle's house.'

John Ericson frowned, obviously taken aback. 'Mr Merton's house? But it's been empty since he died and it was left in rather a mess then.' He leant forward. 'That means it will be cold and dirty,' he said slowly, as though explaining to a child.

'Nevertheless,' said Marla resolutely, 'I assume it's got a roof and a bed, so I would like to stay there. I'm not sure how long I can spend in Cheshire,' she went on by way of explanation, 'so the sooner I can start checking what I have to deal with the better. My father wants me to get everything sorted out before Christmas.'

John Ericson still looked disapproving. 'Well, I know the electricity and water are still connected, but you must remember that we're getting into winter and it will be very cold and extremely uncomfortable there. I strongly recommend a hotel for the night.' Once again, without waiting for an answer, he reached for the telephone on his desk.

'I'll survive,' Marla said crisply before he could pick up the receiver. She stood up. 'If you would please give me the key and then call me a taxi, I'll probably contact you tomorrow.' Her manner made it clear that she was not going to discuss the matter further.

'No need for a taxi,' John Ericson said hastily, also rising. 'Fernwood House is a bit out of the way. I'd better drive you there myself and then at least I can make sure that everything is in working order and the place is habitable.' He looked at her from under surprisingly long lashes, clearly unused to having his advice ignored. 'Are you sure you want to rough it there?'

He shrugged resignedly when she nodded and went through to the outer office, leaving her to think about what he had said. Fernwood House? Marla had been imagining a small cottage, possibly even with a thatched roof, but now she began to have visions of a stately home!

From her first impressions of the solicitor, Marla expected him to drive a respectable family saloon, but he proved to be master of an impressive four-wheel drive. 'I have to visit clients in remote places sometimes,' he explained when he saw her looking at the vehicle. 'I need something that can cover rough ground. Now, instead of driving straight to Fernwood House, shall we make a short detour to a supermarket? I assume you didn't bring any food with you,' he added, looking pointedly at her suitcases.

She reddened, annoyed that this rather arrogant young man should have thought of the necessary shopping before she did. At the supermarket she stocked up on essentials such as bread, butter, milk, and instant coffee. She added some cheese and cereal and decided that would be enough for the time being. Then they set off along country roads which soon narrowed into lanes, and houses grew fewer and fewer. Gazing over the dark, deserted fields, Marla felt apprehensive and homesick for the noise and lights of London.

'Nearly there now,' John Ericson said reassuringly. 'Look, there's Home Farm. Seth Yates lives there. He will be your only neighbour for miles.'

She saw a cluster of buildings with one lighted window and then, about a hundred yards further on, John Ericson braked and stopped.

'We've arrived,' he said, with distinctly false cheerfulness.

Marla's heart sank. The headlights showed neither a mansion nor a cottage, but a small Victorian redbrick house with white trimmings round the gable. The dark porch and the black empty windows looked menacing, and her nerve began to fail. But her companion was already out of the vehicle and striding up the short path. She heard a click as he inserted a key, then a moment later light streamed out as he opened the front door and found the light switch. She swung herself to the ground and followed him into the house, where she found him opening the doors leading off a small hall, switching more lights on and off.

'That's the sitting-room,' he told her, pointing at one door. 'It doesn't look as if it was used much.' He opened another door and the light went on. 'Ah. The kitchen.' He looked round almost approvingly. 'This is obviously where he spent most of his time.'

The painted wooden cupboards looked as if they had been there since the house was built. There was a ceramic sink with a wooden draining board and a small gas stove, and a scrubbed pine table stood in the centre of the stone-flagged floor, but the most prominent feature was the large cast-iron stove filled with white ash. In front of it were a rag mat and a big armchair upholstered in worn black leather with an old tartan blanket thrown casually across it. There were some dishes on the draining board, and apart from the low temperature and hint of damp the room gave the impression that its owner had just left it for some reason and would soon be coming back. To one side of the hearth was a basket with a well-worn cushion in it. John Ericson looked at this with curiosity.

'Nobody said he had a pet,' he commented. 'I wonder what happened to it?'

Marla turned on the sink taps. They were stiff and she was relieved when water finally gushed out. While the solicitor brought in her cases and provisions she hurried up the steep flight of stairs. There were three bedrooms, one of them with a double bed with the sheets thrown back as if the occupant had just got up. Another had a bed with a bare mattress, while the third was piled with cardboard

28

boxes. There was a tiny bathroom with a rust-stained bath, but the toilet did flush when she reached up and pulled the chain. She went back downstairs where John Ericson waited with obvious impatience for her decision.

'Well? What do you think of it? Now you've seen it, wouldn't you rather find somewhere in town?'

She shook her head, though without enthusiasm. 'I can cope here. There's all that I need for a short stay and I don't expect to be here for long. I intend to be gone before Christmas.'

'Well, if you're sure . . . '

'I'm sure.'

After the visit to the supermarket she knew she really had no option; that she could not afford a hotel room.

He was glancing at his watch, obviously deciding that he'd done enough for a foolish young woman who wouldn't take his advice.

'In that case, can I leave you? I'm due somewhere in half an hour.'

'Please, I'll be all right by myself.'

He surprised her by taking her hand in his and looking at her with his blue eyes full of genuine concern. 'Suppose something goes wrong?'

'I have my mobile.'

'Promise you'll call me if you need help. I'll leave you my card.'

She nodded and gently withdrew her hand. 'Thank you for all your help. I'll see you soon.'

'You definitely will. I'll probably drive out here sometime so you don't have to make the trip into town if you don't want to. It would be difficult anyway. I think there are only a couple of buses a day which come this way.'

He went out the front door but reappeared within seconds, holding out a black bag. 'Your handbag, I presume? You left it in my car.'

She reddened. 'I'm sorry. I'm always doing that.'

When the sound of his engine had died away, Marla turned back into the little house. She locked the front door and returned to the kitchen where she took a quick look in one of the cupboards, but found it was almost empty except for some tins of cat food. She sighed. If things got really desperate perhaps she could live on curried cat food, if she could find some curry powder!

Reluctantly she took her coat off, shivered, and was glad to find a very battered tin kettle so she could boil enough water on the old-fashioned gas stove for a cup of coffee, and then she made herself a cheese sandwich. She ate this light supper snuggled into the armchair, which was definitely comfortable and welcoming. Afterwards she went to put the perishable food away in the small refrigerator, but recoiled at the sight and smell of the various packets of food and the very over-ripe cheese it contained. Hastily she picked up these items at arm's length and put them out in the garden.

She switched off the kitchen lights and took a kettleful of hot water up to the bathroom where she undressed, washed rapidly, put on her night clothes, and then added a warm jumper on top of them. She suspected that the unmade bed in the main bedroom was as it had been left when Uncle Andrew got up for the last time, so she snuggled down on the bare mattress in the other bedroom under the protection of her coat. She expected a long and sleepless night and lay for some time staring at the ceiling, wishing she was back in Mrs Savage's bed-sit, but it had been an exhausting day, and eventually she fell asleep.

2

She woke abruptly, threw back her coat, sat up and gazed bleary-eyed around at the bleak little room, involuntarily clasping her arms round her as the cold hit her. Gradually she remembered where she was and at the same time became aware that she had been disturbed by a loud knocking on the front door. She fumbled for her watch. Eight o'clock! Surely the young solicitor wasn't calling this early?

The knocking continued implacably. She slipped her bare feet into her shoes, shrugged her coat on over her pyjamas, went downstairs and reluctantly opened the door a crack and peered out. The young man on the doorstep grinned and held out a package. 'Hi! I'm your neighbour, Seth Yates from Home Farm. I've brought you some eggs as a welcoming present.'

He was not only young, he was also tall, well-built and good-looking. He had curly black hair, and when he smiled white teeth flashed in a tanned face.

Marla opened the door a little further and automatically stretched out a hand to accept the package; then, acutely aware of her own appearance, hastily retreated into the shelter of the hall. 'Thank you,' she managed. 'I'm Marla Merton and I'd offer you a coffee, but as you can see I'm not very organised at the moment.'

Instead of taking the hint and leaving, the young man followed her into the hall and strode past her into the kitchen, leaving her to trail behind him. 'No problem,' he said cheerfully over his shoulder, already reaching for the tap. 'I know where the kettle is. Why don't you go and get dressed while I make the coffee?'

He had left Marla no choice. Were all Cheshire men so domineering? She fled upstairs, rinsed her face in cold water and changed hastily into yesterday's jeans and sweater, combed her hair, and came downstairs prepared to be very frosty towards this stranger who was making himself at home in her kitchen. However, it was difficult to keep this resolution when she was greeted not only by the smell of coffee but also by a plate of hot buttered toast. Her visitor was already crunching a half-slice. Marla sank down opposite him at the kitchen table.

'Your solicitor told me when I met him in town yesterday morning that you would be coming soon,' Seth Yates informed her. 'I heard his car last night and saw the light in the bedroom afterwards so I guessed you were here. So you're Andrew Merton's great-niece.'

'You were friends with my great-uncle?'

'Not exactly friends, but we were neighbours, and as he got older I was able to help him when he needed it.' A shadow crossed his face. 'I was the one who found him here in the kitchen when he had his stroke. The light didn't

35

come on in the evening so I came to see if anything was the matter. He was unconscious on the floor; apparently had been for several hours. I called the ambulance, but he died in hospital later that night.'

'I never met him,' Marla remarked. 'My father said he'd only seen him once, so we don't know much about him.'

'It was quite a surprise when we learned that he had any family. He never mentioned relatives. Well, he liked his own company and spent most of his time walking and reading.' He put his cup down. 'What are you planning to do now you are here?'

Marla shrugged. 'I'm not busy at the moment.' This was a polite way she had used before of saying she was unemployed. 'My father asked me to come and look at the place and see what I could do to get it ready to be sold.'

'You're going to sell it?' Seth said sharply.

'What else can we do with it? It's not as if I live in this part of England, and my parents are settled in Spain. Why?'

He was looking very discouraging. 'You might have difficulty selling it. It needs a lot of work doing to it. I used to point things out to Mr Merton, but he always said it would last his lifetime — and so it did.'

Marla heaved a sigh. The outlook was bleak. 'I could see last night that it was in a bit of a mess, but at least I can tidy it up.' She shivered. 'And it's cold after being empty for weeks. Where did Great-uncle keep the coal?'

Seth stared at her. 'Coal?' He gestured at the ashes in the stove. 'That's a wood-burning stove. I used to keep Mr Merton supplied with wood from the farm, and once you get that stove going it will heat the house.' He stood up and stretched, his fingers almost reaching the ceiling. 'Shall we see if he's left any wood? I can show you where he kept other things as well.'

'That would be a help — but don't you have to get back to your farm?' Marla had a townswoman's impression that all farmers worked on the land from dawn to dusk, but Seth was shaking his head.

'I don't have stock to attend to. Apart from a few chickens, I grow things, and a field of cabbages can wait for a bit.'

His hand rested briefly on her shoulder and she was aware of its warmth as he guided her to a lean-to where the wood was stored. There was still a small pile in one corner, and as he brought in an armful of logs a large black-and-white cat strolled in the open kitchen door behind him and made for the cat basket, where it curled up snugly and lay surveying the kitchen with a lordly air.

'Theo!' exclaimed Seth. 'I wondered where he'd got to. He vanished after Mr Merton was taken away. He's probably been terrorising every cat in the neighbourhood since then and pinching their food.'

'But he can't stay here!' Marla exclaimed. 'I don't know anything about cats, and I don't expect to be here for long.'

Seth laughed as he knelt to open the stove door. 'Try explaining that to Theo. All you have to do is feed him occasionally and let him out at night. Now, let me find a bucket and shovel.'

He was quick and purposeful and soon the ashes had been removed and the fire lit.

'Just keep topping it up with the occasional log,' he instructed her, 'and you won't have any trouble. It will give you hot water as well. I'll bring you some more wood when I get a chance. Now, anything else I can do for you?'

'I think you've done plenty,' Marla said with real gratitude. Warmth and hot water would make a big difference, but she was anxious now to be left on her own so that she could examine her little kingdom in detail.

This time Seth accepted his dismissal. 'If you do want any help, just come and tell me,' he said, and he left.

She watched him striding down the lane. At least she had a very helpful and attractive neighbour, but she would have to be careful not to let him take over. She turned slowly back into the house. The kitchen was already heating up nicely. As she wondered what to do next, she saw Theo and, wondering how long it was since the cat had eaten, she opened one of the tins of cat food and put half of it in a dish which she put on the floor near the cat. For a few seconds he ignored it, but as she turned away he slipped out of his nest and was soon devouring the food and she was satisfied that she had done something right.

'Listen to me,' she said, hands on hips as she addressed the cat. 'I'll feed you when I can afford it, but that's all. Understood?'

He padded back to his basket, curled up and went to sleep, ignoring her completely. With a whole unfamiliar house to explore, Marla began with a feeling of excitement, wondering what she would discover about her unknown great-uncle. First she found in the kitchen cupboards an adequate but not extensive store of well-used utensils.

Between the kitchen and the back door was a short passage with a small cloakroom filled with old coats, shoes and rubber boots, and on the other side was a walk-in larder whose cold stone floor and stone shelves offered a good storage space for fresh food. Outside was a tool shed, though the small back garden gave few signs of cultivation.

The sitting room was neat, but was obviously rarely used. Ornaments stood on a sideboard which contained what was clearly the 'best' (and therefore rarely used) crockery and glassware. The wardrobe and chest of drawers in the main bedroom held her great-uncle's small collection of practical clothes, and she was not yet ready to explore the cardboard boxes. If they had been left untouched for years there could be little of interest in them.

Having completed her tour of inspection, Marla went downstairs slowly. The house had been an ideal home for an unsociable bachelor, but that was about all that could be said for it. It was old-fashioned and neglected, and needed a thorough turn-out.

She reclaimed from the garden the various containers which she had found in the refrigerator, throwing most of them in the dustbin. The cheese had vanished and she wondered whether it was Theo or mice who had eaten it.

It was getting on for lunchtime by the time she had finished her inspection, and Marla looked at her meagre resources. She could have egg on toast for lunch, cheese on toast for tea, and then repeat the menu the following day. It was not a cheering prospect. Just as she had located a rather rusty cast-iron frying pan, there was a knock at the door, and she groaned. Not Seth Yates again so soon! How could she discourage him?

But this time it was John Ericson who stood outside, and he was clutching a large cardboard box. 'This isn't a business visit,' he assured her. 'I told my Mother last night that you had come to stay here and she insisted on sending you a few things to tide you over until you're ready to go shopping properly.' He held out the box. 'Here, with my mother's compliments.'

He opened the top so that she could see that the box contained various tins and jars. She was eager to take it and start exploring but she looked at John anxiously. 'Thank your mother very much — but you must let me pay her for it.'

'Certainly not. You are a client, and it's a gift to welcome you,' he said firmly. She stood aside as he carried the box into the kitchen and put it on the table. He looked round and gave a mock shudder. 'What do you think of it so far?'

'It's — adequate,' she conceded, 'but it doesn't live up to its grand name.'

'Fernwood House? Well, apparently a long time ago there was a very splendid house on this site, but its owners supported King Charles and it was burned down by Roundheads during the Civil War. When this house was built in Victorian times the rather snobbish owner decided

43

to use the old name. Now, is there anything I can do for you?'

'Thank you, but the farmer, Mr Yates, called this morning and lit the stove. I've looked through the house, and I think I can cope now.'

'Seth's been round already, has he? He didn't waste any time! Why aren't I surprised? Then I'll leave you to settle in for now, but we've still got things to discuss another time,' he reminded her.

He drove off, leaving her free to examine the contents of the box. There were tins of soup, spaghetti and beans, a large loaf and two jars of obviously homemade jam. Marla's spirits lifted. Then her eyes widened and she nearly dropped a jar of jam. The boxful of food was charity! She had been given the food because John Ericson had realised how hard up she was! He had seen how little Marla had bought at the supermarket and that, together with her question about how soon Uncle Andrew's money would be available, must have given him a clue how desperate she was

44

for money. He had told his mother, who had decided the newcomer could do with a little help, but the matter had been managed very tactfully and on reflection she was too pleased and relieved to feel insulted. Anyway, she was nearly broke.

Her life as an actress and model meant that Marla, used to living in temporarily rented rooms, never stayed long enough to put down roots, but she had learned the importance of keeping things clean and tidy in a small space and the afternoon was spent sweeping floors and dusting, shaking rugs out of doors and cleaning windows, a task which Uncle Andrew had obviously neglected.

By tea-time she was tired but pleasantly aware that her surroundings were definitely looking better. She fed Theo again and as she settled down in the armchair after a quick meal she could hear him purring loudly. She looked round. What could she do with the rest of the evening now darkness had fallen? Her great-uncle had not acquired a television set and his radio crackled and hissed when she turned it on. The books she could find were to do with natural history and, somewhat surprisingly, cricket, and there was also a collection of English detective novels.

Then a tinkling burst of music could be heard. Theo stopped purring and looked round aggressively, but Marla was fumbling in her handbag for her mobile phone. It was her father.

'I just called to see everything is all right. What's the house like?'

'It's an ugly, run-down Victorian cottage,' she told him. 'It's definitely not going to sell for a fortune.'

'Oh, well,' said her father philosophically. 'I didn't expect anything, so even a few thousand will be a nice bonus. And the contents?'

'Basic and boring, but I'll get rid of them somehow.'

'Do your best. Love from both of us.' And her father rang off.

Easy for him to say. He didn't realise

what a difficult task he had given her.

She looked at her mobile, then decided she needed sympathy and understanding. A glance at her watch showed that it was too early yet for actors to be worrying about the evening's performance and she rapidly dialled a number. After three rings she heard a familiar voice.

'Hello?'

'Sasha, it's me, Marla.'

There was a yelp from the other end. 'Marla! I was thinking of you a few minutes ago.'

'How are you doing? Last time I rang you said you'd got some good reviews.'

There was a pause, and the reply was despondent. 'I got some good reviews, but the play didn't. We're closing at the end of the week.'

'Oh, I am sorry!'

'It happens. How about you? Have you sold many cars?'

'I'm not at the motor show any longer. I'm deep in the country.' She gave a rapid explanation of what had brought her to Cheshire.

There was a thoughtful pause. 'You mean you're all by yourself in a house which needs cleaning and tidying? You'd probably be glad to offer free board to a friend who was willing to help with the scrubbing.'

Marla did not hesitate. 'Yes! How soon can you get here?'

'Three days — two, if Esmeralda behaves.'

'Here's the address.'

Sasha and Marla had met at drama school, become firm friends and kept in contact ever since, sometimes finding work together. Sasha was the opposite of Marla — small, bubbly and blonde. She was also a good actress, one of the few students who obviously had the potential to make a good living on the stage, and she had spent the past few years working in provincial theatres while hoping for the breakthrough that would take her to London and success. The play in which she had been touring should have done that. It was a light comedy and starred a man who had appeared in a successful television series for a couple of years. It had been thought that his fans would flock to see him in the flesh, but something had clearly gone wrong and Marla was happy to be able to offer her friend a roof over her head till something else turned up. She looked forward to Sasha's arrival in Esmeralda, an old and much-loved car which the two girls had painted bright green one weekend in an unsuccessful attempt to cover up its rust patches.

Marla was cheered at the prospect of Sasha's company and support in these unfamiliar surroundings, but meanwhile she had to deal with the young, arrogant solicitor and prove to him that she was intelligent and competent enough to deal with Andrew Merton's property. In the tool shed she had found a very old bicycle. It was some years since she had ridden off to school each day on a bicycle and she regarded the aged machine dubiously, but it was intact and the next morning, having pumped up its tyres and oiled it generously, she decided she could risk riding it into Woodham. She was glad that no one saw her first uncertain, wobbling attempts to ride it along the lanes, but she did succeed in reaching the small town safely, and wheeled it up to the solicitor's office with great relief, congratulating herself on surviving the journey. Beryl the receptionist looked at her vehicle with distaste.

'You can't bring that machine in here,' she said firmly. 'Leave it outside the door.'

'But suppose someone steals it,' Marla objected.

Beryl's eyebrows rose. 'I doubt if anyone will want that object,' she said coldly. 'Incidentally, shouldn't you be wearing a helmet?'

'I'm going to get one today,' Marla said, abandoning the bike to its fate. 'Can I see Mr John Ericson?'

'He is very busy today. Have you an appointment?'

'No, but he said we had to discuss things . . . '

'So I did,' said a voice. John Ericson appeared at his office door. Marla shook the hand he held out, conscious that there might still be traces of oil on hers. This was confirmed when he took out a handkerchief and fastidiously wiped his palm.

'I see you've got your own transport,' he remarked. 'At least it will be better than waiting hours for a bus. Now, come in my office. You're lucky,' he informed her. 'I've got twenty minutes before my next appointment.'

Marla followed him, conscious of Beryl glaring at her retreating back. 'I don't think your receptionist likes me,' she murmured.

'She sees it as her job to protect me,' John Ericson told her, looking through a pile of files and picking one out. 'Now, this is what we have to discuss . . . '

There were various points, but he explained them clearly and briefly, pausing for questions. There seemed to be no major obstacles to Marla arranging to sell the house.

'Of course, until it's actually sold there are certain expenses,' John Ericson pointed out. 'There's council tax and insurance, as well as the cost of any fuel you may use. However, roughly four hundred pounds will be transferred to your bank account sometime in the near future.' He looked at her. 'I will try to hurry up the transfer.'

Marla was delighted to hear this. The money and free accommodation at the house would keep her going for a few weeks, and after that there was sure to be some kind of work available around Christmas. After signing various papers she reclaimed her bike, which had been rejected by any would-be bicycle thieves, and rode home happily to spend the afternoon finishing the task of cleaning and tidying the kitchen. In the evening she curled up with one of the detective novels before retreating to her bed, which was now properly made up with blankets and sheets which she had found in a cupboard.

There was a definite satisfaction to

be gained from creating a better environment in the neglected house, and she surveyed the result of her labours with pleasure the next morning before she set to work again. But it was tiring, and she was not too upset when a knock on the door interrupted her. It was Seth Yates, her farmer neighbour, and once again he had caught her looking far from her best. She pushed her hair back from a sweaty forehead with her red, wet hands and hastily pulled off the old towel she had fastened round her as an improvised apron. Once again he was holding out a small package.

'I had to get rid of one of my surplus cockerels,' he said, 'but a whole chicken is too much for me, so I thought you might like these.'

Marla was used to neatly packaged meat from the supermarket and unwrapped the parcel gingerly, exclaiming with delight when she found that 'these' were two plump chicken breasts. Delectable fresh meat! She and Sasha would enjoy the treat.

'Thank you!' she exclaimed. 'They look gorgeous, and just right for a meal for two.'

She saw the white teeth as his grin widened, and suddenly realised that he had brought her the two breasts hoping to be invited to share them with her, and now he was assuming that his ploy had been successful and that she was about to invite him to be her guest. This was awkward!

'I've got a friend coming to stay,' she said hastily. 'I can cook these for the two of us.'

The grin had vanished and his face had set bleakly. 'A friend?'

'Yes — Sasha. She's arriving in the next day or two.'

The tension left his face and he was smiling again. 'A girl friend? At least she will be company for you.'

Had he thought she was intending to import a boyfriend? Fernwood House in its present state was scarcely the setting for a love nest.

'She's going to help me clean and

tidy the house,' Marla told him. Trying to think of a safe subject of conversation, she remembered something that John Ericson had said. 'Is it true that there used to be another, bigger house on this site a long time ago?'

Seth nodded. 'Indeed there was. There was a manor house here for centuries, the centre of a large estate. My farm was the nearest to it, so that is why it is called Home Farm.'

'But it burnt down?'

His face darkened. 'It was burnt down, destroyed, by the Roundheads opposing Charles the First. The family who had owned it for hundreds of years were reduced to comparative poverty and had to sell most of their land.'

'And the Victorian builders gave this the old name, Fernwood House?'

He was laughing again. 'Well, they could scarcely call it Number One, Rosehill Lane, when there isn't even a Number Two!'

'How long did Uncle Andrew live here? It is odd to be in his house, and yet I know nothing about him, and I haven't found any clues.'

'He was here about eight or nine years, I think. I was away at college for a lot of the time, and I only really got to know him when I took over the farm from my parents.' He frowned. 'I don't know where he was before that. Apparently he arrived here one day in a hired van, unloaded a lot of boxes, and that was that. He never talked about his life before he came here.'

He left soon afterwards, after checking that the stove was still burning and that she did not require any more help, but he urged her again to call on him if there were any problems. Afterwards Marla decided the kitchen had received enough attention for the time being. She had only given the unused sitting room a cursory examination before, so now she went to examine it more thoroughly and she could not help noticing how impersonal it was. There were china and tarnished brass ornaments on the sideboard and mantelpiece, but the only interesting object was a sepia photograph of Fernwood House obviously taken in the early years of the twentieth century, judging by the clothes worn by the couple standing proudly in front of the house. The house looked very spruce with rose bushes each side of the door, and Marla reflected grimly on the effort it would take to restore the house to that condition. But there were no recent photographs, no mementoes of family or friends, no hint of Andrew Merton's earlier life. Oh well, perhaps all such souvenirs were packed away in the cardboard boxes in the small bedroom. Uncle Andrew would not be the only person who had never got round to unpacking everything after moving home.

Soon afterwards her mobile phone rang. It was Sasha, announcing her imminent arrival. Marla raced round putting fresh bedclothes on both beds. She had barely finished when a car horn sounded outside and she saw the bright green of Esmeralda by the front door and ran outside to greet her friend. They embraced warmly, and then Marla stood back and waved at the house.

'Welcome to my stately home. First impressions?'

Sasha looked and wrinkled her nose, obviously not filled with instant admiration. 'Well, it's got a roof and a front door so I assume it's got a kitchen as well, and I'm dying for a cup of tea.'

Marla produced tea and toast and Sasha accepted them gratefully. Her friend noticed that she looked tired, and there were shadows under her eyes. 'Been having a hard time?' she asked sympathetically, and Sasha sipped her tea and then nodded emphatically.

'Our so-called leading man, Gordon Towers, the great television star, thought he only had to walk on stage and smile and all his adoring fans would be happy. The idea of learning his lines, let alone trying to act, seemed to come as a shock to him. Then, after a few audiences had given him a very cool reception, he started to have a few drinks before each performance and that didn't help. The rest of us were trying to compensate for his lack of effort and cover up his mistakes, but it was very difficult. Of course, when it was announced that we would not be transferring to the theatre in London he decided that it was the fault of everybody except him, and there was a very nasty atmosphere for the last few performances.' She heaved a deep sigh. 'So it was goodbye to my dream of appearing in the West End, being noticed by some well-known director, and becoming a star.'

'It will happen,' Marla assured her. 'You've got genuine talent and it's bound to be recognised eventually.'

Sasha tried to smile. 'I hope so. I've already contacted a few people who may have work to offer fairly soon, so I'll just have to wait and see. What about you?'

Marla shrugged. 'Well, I've finally accepted that I'm no good as an actress, I can't earn enough to live on as a model, and after hitting a possible customer I don't think I'll be offered much work as a demonstrator. Staying in this house till I've arranged its sale has given me a respite, so I'll just have to think of some other career — like rocket scientist or brain surgeon.'

They both giggled. This was not the first time they had had to cheer each other up when the future looked bleak for both. 'Come on,' said Marla. 'Finish your tea and I'll give you the tour of the house.'

Sasha didn't make any comments as she was shown the house. Back in the warmth of the kitchen, Marla looked at her friend challengingly. 'Well?'

Sasha shrugged. 'It reminds me of some of the digs we've stayed in. It's adequate, but I wouldn't want to stay here permanently.'

'That's how I feel. However, the plan at the moment is to clean it up, make it as presentable as possible, and then sell it. So with luck I'll only be here for a few weeks and then I can return to the comforts of London.'

Sasha was frowning. 'I wouldn't want

to live here because it's such a long way from the town and any shops, and plenty of other people will feel the same way. If you had an emergency and needed help, who could you go to? Did I see another building a little way back?'

'There's a farm — Home Farm — about a hundred yards away. A young man, Seth Yates, is the only person living there.'

Sasha lifted an enquiring eyebrow. 'One young man, eh? What's he like?'

Marla allowed a slow smile to grow. 'Rather attractive. He's already called round a couple of times. In fact you'll be eating his chicken for your supper.'

'He seems to have impressed you, and if he's willing to give you free chicken he must like you as well. Do you fancy him?'

'Well, I like what I've seen so far, and he does seem keen to help me.'

'Keep me informed of any developments.'

They enjoyed their chicken supper before an early bedtime. Marla was relieved that she could assure Sasha that Uncle Andrew had died in hospital and not in the bed she was given.

The next morning the two of them continued to clean the house. At one point Sasha, who was washing the outside window frames, called Marla. 'Come and look at this,' she said grimly, poking at a window frame which crumbled under the pressure. 'It's completely rotten, and I don't think the others are much better. They all need replacing.'

'Well I'm not going to have it done. We're just going to have to price it very low so we can find a quick buyer,' Marla sighed. 'It's not the most exciting place to live in and I don't want to spend long here. I've set myself the target of being gone by Christmas.'

She realised that Sasha wasn't listening. Instead she was staring wide-eyed at something coming along the lane. Marla turned to see what was attracting her attention and blinked. Had she suddenly been transported back in time? Riding towards them on a black horse was a Royalist Cavalier, a typical follower of Charles I, complete from large feathered hat to spurred boots, a sword hanging by his side. Nearing the two girls, he brought the horse to a halt, dismounted in one smooth movement, and swept off his wide-brimmed hat in a low bow, revealing himself as Seth Yates.

'Greetings, fair ladies,' he said solemnly.

'What on earth . . . ?' Marla began.

'I'm a member of the Sealed Knot,' he explained. 'We recreate Civil War battles. I'm going to a meeting today, and I couldn't resist showing myself off in all my glory.'

'I'm glad you did. It's fascinating,' she said, looking at the wide lace collar and embroidered sash. She remembered her friend, who stood eyeing the newcomer. 'Oh, let me introduce you to Sasha, the friend I mentioned who will be staying with me for a while.'

Seth turned to Sasha and there was a

long silence as they looked at each other, both unsmiling, wary. 'I hope you enjoy your stay,' Seth said at last, just as Marla was beginning to wonder what was the matter.

Sasha gave a brief nod. 'I expect I will.'

Sasha's usual lively, friendly manner seemed to have vanished. Neither of the two seemed prepared to say anything more to each other and Marla desperately sought for something to talk about.

'We hope to finish the cleaning and tidying in a couple of days,' she said brightly. 'Can you recommend an estate agent?'

Seth's head swivelled towards her. 'Do you want one so soon? I hoped you were going to stay here for a few weeks at least,' he said in a voice tinged with dismay. Marla felt flattered. He obviously didn't want her to go!

'It depends how things turn out,' she said vaguely.

He nodded, and then turned to his horse. 'Well, you'll find a big agent in the High Street. Now I'll have to leave you, or I'll be late for the meeting.' He swung himself back into the saddle and once again saluted her. 'Farewell, Mistress Marla.' He gave a quick glance at Sasha. 'Goodbye, ma'am.'

Then he was gone, riding off down the lane. Marla looked after him. 'Doesn't he look gorgeous?' she said. When there was no reply she turned to her friend. 'Didn't you like him?'

Sasha shrugged. 'He seemed all right. A bit conceited, perhaps, showing himself off, dressing up like a kid.'

'You're an actress and you dress up all the time,' Marla reminded her.

'That's different. I do it to earn a living.'

'He looked splendid, and I'm glad he came,' Marla said quickly, feeling bound to defend her neighbour, and puzzled at the mutually antagonistic reaction she had sensed between Seth and Sasha.

'Well, he obviously likes you as much as you like him.'

This did seem pretty clear, and Marla

felt her self-esteem was definitely boosted. She wondered idly why Seth had become a Cavalier with the Sealed Knot. Was it the contrast between the literally down-to-earth life of a farmer and the glamour of the elaborate costume of a follower of King Charles?

3

No more was said about Seth, and the two girls worked steadily away until finally they had done all they could.

'At least you can live in it now without worrying about creepy-crawlies in the corners,' Sasha said. 'What's the next job?'

'I suppose we ought to see what's in the boxes in the small bedroom,' sighed Marla. 'But if Uncle Andrew didn't open them for ten years there can't be anything very interesting in them.'

'Maybe there was nothing for him, but after ten years it will all be vintage, retro. Let's have a look.'

The first box they opened was full of domestic equipment which a man on his own was unlikely to need. There was a complete dinner service in fine china, quite unlike the random collection of plates in the kitchen. Another box held sheets and blankets.

'Good! I found sufficient for one single bed and just enough for the double but we could do with more. These will come in useful when we've washed them.'

Two more boxes were full of men's clothing — suits and ties and smart shirts which would have looked very out of place in the country. Marla shook her head, puzzled.

'These must have been expensive in their time. Everything we've found so far seems to indicate that Uncle Andrew lived a very different life before he came here. He must have had a larger house, better furnished, probably in a town, and whatever he did required him to dress smartly.'

'And he didn't live alone!' Sasha said. 'Look here!' She had opened another box, one of the larger ones, and now she was holding up a woman's dress. Marla stared as Sasha plunged into the box, pulling out armfuls of clothing. There was a complete woman's wardrobe scattered on the floor by the time she had finished — underwear, dresses, skirts and jumpers, a jacket and even a pair of court shoes.

'They're not designer, but they are good quality,' Sasha said, surveying them with an expert's eyes. 'They're outdated now, of course. I should say they are about ten to fifteen years old.'

'So something happened before he came here,' Marla said slowly. 'I wonder what it was? He must have cared about the woman, anyway, or he wouldn't have kept her clothes.'

'Are you sure there aren't any clues elsewhere in the house?' Sasha demanded. 'No letters or photographs, no wedding certificate?'

'Nothing that gives the slightest clue to his life before he bought this house.'

'Maybe the solicitor you told me about knows something.'

'He may do. I'll ask him next time I see him. Meanwhile, let's put the clothes back in the box for the time being.'

They tidied up and went downstairs to prepare their evening meal. Their food supply was running low; Mrs Ericson's tins were nearly exhausted.

'We'd better go shopping tomorrow,' Marla commented, surveying the nearly empty refrigerator, now clean and sweet-smelling. 'The only trouble is, I haven't got much money left to buy anything.'

'You can have what I've got, but I'm running out as well,' Sasha confessed. 'My credit card has reached its limit. I had to pay cash for Esmeralda's petrol so I could get here.'

'Let's see what we've got.'

They looked through their purses, bags and pockets and put all that they found on the kitchen table. It made a depressingly small pile, with more coins than notes.

'There's enough for essentials,' frowned Marla, 'but what do we do after that? As I told you, I'm supposed to get the remaining money from Uncle Andrew's bank account fairly soon, but I don't know how long it will be before that is sorted out.'

Sasha gazed round the room. 'Your father did tell you to clear the house. Isn't there something here you can sell?' She brightened up. 'You've seen enough television programmes about antiques. There could be some very valuable item somewhere in the house that an antique dealer would pay good money for. It could be worth thousands! You'd be rich!'

'Don't get carried away,' warned Marla. 'There are all those things in the sitting room, of course, but I think they are all junk.'

'Let's check. Remember to look at the marks underneath and check the condition.'

But an hour's careful search simply confirmed Marla's first impression. The ornaments were crude, cheap items, very unlikely to make an antique collector's heart beat faster. Gloomily the two girls returned to the warmth of the kitchen.

'You were right,' Sasha said. 'It's all rubbish. Either they were left by the previous owner or he probably picked them up at car-boot sales to try and cheer the room up a bit.' She stopped and sat up straight. 'A car-boot sale! We could sell them there, and a lot of other stuff! Where do they have car-boot sales round here?'

'I don't know,' confessed Marla, 'but we could buy a local paper when we go shopping tomorrow. That would tell us.'

'Right! We'll start clearing the house and we'll be able to eat on the proceeds.' She waved at Theo, who had just stalked into the kitchen. 'We'll be able to feed the cat as well. His tins are nearly all gone.'

Esmeralda reluctantly sputtered into life the next morning and Sasha was frowning as she carefully reversed into the lane.

'I hate to say this, but I think Esmeralda is getting too old to go on working much longer.'

'Has she passed her MOT?' Marla enquired suspiciously, but Sasha nodded virtuously.

'Oh, yes, a few weeks ago. I made

friends with this very nice mechanic and he gave Esmeralda a good overhaul so that she passed the test. He did say that some of his work could be called emergency repairs, however, and he couldn't guarantee them for too long.'

They made it safely to Woodham and luckily found a parking place near the solicitors' office. 'Let's call in and see if they know anything about this woman whose clothes we found,' Marla suggested. 'His dragon of a receptionist might not let me pass because I haven't got an appointment, but we can try.'

The receptionist, Miss Richards, did indeed greet her with an icy stare.

'Mr Ericson cannot see you now, Miss Merton,' she said curtly. 'He is with a client.'

Marla's shoulders sagged. 'Could I wait till he's finished?'

'I don't think he will have time to help you then . . . '

She was interrupted by Sasha's squeal. 'Oh! But you look as if you could help me! I desperately need a good hairdresser, and you obviously go to one . . . '

Beryl Richards's hand automatically went to her neat head, but then she bristled. 'I am here as a receptionist, not to give out beauty tips!'

Sasha looked at her pleadingly. 'But I really need to know. I'm an actress and I expect to have an interview with an important producer soon, and I'll have to make a good impression.'

Beryl visibly wavered, and as she did so John Ericson's door opened and an elderly gentleman emerged, followed by John.

'If you need any more advice, just phone me,' the young solicitor was saying before he saw Marla and stopped in mid-sentence. 'Miss Merton!'

'I wanted to ask you a couple of questions, if it's not too inconvenient,' she said.

'Just a second.'

He ushered the elderly man to the door, said goodbye and then returned, glancing at his watch. 'This time I've got five minutes, that's all,' he warned her.

'That should be enough.' She followed him into his office, avoiding Beryl's glare, and they sat down. She told him briefly about their discovery of the woman's clothing.

'And what do you think I can do?' he enquired impatiently.

'I was wondering if you could tell me anything about her. Was it his wife?'

John was shaking his head. 'I'm afraid I don't know. Your uncle never said a word about his life before he came to Woodham. He bought the house and its contents at an auction after its previous owner died suddenly. He did leave an envelope of documents with us for safe keeping together with his will and instructions what to do in the event of his death.' He looked at her, making her uncomfortably aware that she had not thought to enquire what had happened to her dead relative's remains. 'He was cremated, and his ashes scattered as he requested.

He seemed eager to leave as little trace after death as he had in life. When I looked at the documents there was only his birth certificate, the deeds of the house, details of his bank account, and your father's name and address. The address was out of date, in fact, and I had some trouble before I traced him to Spain.'

'But what did he live on? Was he retired? If he had a pension, who did he work for?'

Again John Ericson was shaking his head. 'Of course he had his social security pension, and occasionally he would pay a few hundred in cash into his bank account, but I don't know where that came from because there was no indication in the paperwork.' He stopped, looking at her troubled face. 'I'm sorry, Miss Merton. Obviously I was curious about him, but I had no reason, no justification, to try and find out more.' His tone made it clear that he did not see it as part of his duties to satisfy her idle curiosity.

She managed to smile and stood up. 'Well, thank you for telling me. I suppose I'm just being too inquisitive.'

He came round the desk to see her to the door. 'I'm glad you came to me, that you see me as a source of information.' He nodded at the outer office. 'Is that blonde a friend?'

'Yes. She's staying with me for a bit.'

'Well, let's hope Beryl hasn't eaten her alive.'

But instead of the frosty atmosphere they had expected, they found Beryl Richards and Sasha seated side by side, each holding a cup of coffee and chatting like old friends. Sasha stood up as Marla emerged from the office with John, and Beryl's face fell.

'Must you go?' she said sadly, but Sasha nodded.

'We've got things to do and things to buy,' she said.

'Well, you must come back soon and we'll have another talk,' the receptionist sighed.

'Of course I will — and I might have

something for you.'

Beryl's eyes sparkled, though her farewell to Marla was still cool.

Outside in the street, Marla turned to Sasha. 'What did you do to that woman?' she marvelled.

Sasha looked smug. 'The old tried-and-tested technique. You heard me tell her that I needed to have my hair done and look good because I'm an actress. That always gets people interested. She asked me if I'd ever met anyone famous and it turned out that she is a great fan of Gordon Towers, the television star I've been working with.'

'You can't have told her the truth about him or she wouldn't have been so happy.'

'Of course not. I wasn't going to ruin her illusions. I gave her lots of inside information about him — his favourite foods, where he buys his clothes — and I managed to give the impression that he was the most charming man I'd ever met. It just shows what a good actress I am!'

'And what are you going to take her?'

'A signed photo of Mr Towers. He insisted on giving them to all the cast when he first met us. He actually thought we'd be grateful!' She paused. 'I did notice that when she wasn't asking questions about Gordon, she was asking about you, but I couldn't find out why she found you so interesting. Now, did you get any more information about the mystery woman?'

Marla shook her head. 'Uncle Andrew was definitely a very secretive man. Even the ornaments and pictures came with the house and don't show his personal taste.'

'So nothing has a family connection and you can sell everything with an easy conscience. Let's find somewhere to buy the local paper.'

Sasha looked up and down the street, which they had discovered was unimaginatively called Main Street, and shrugged her shoulders. 'Well, I wouldn't come here for a shopping spree because it's no Oxford Street, that's for sure, but presumably there is a newsagent's.'

They soon found one and bought a paper. Combing through the small ads, they discovered details of a car-boot sale to be held at a local community centre on the following Sunday.

'You don't have to book, you just turn up,' Marla noted.

'At six o'clock in the morning!' Sasha said gloomily. 'Oh well, I suppose we can survive that.'

Back at the house they started to sort out what they could take to the sale. It was easy to decide that all the china figurines and brass ashtrays should go from the sitting room, together with the books. Linen runners embroidered with crude flowers could also go. Then what? There was some very old-fashioned kitchen paraphernalia which Sasha declared hopefully was probably collectable, basins and baking trays, and a boxed set of fish-knives which did not look as if they had ever been used. Some of the contents of the boxes from the bedroom, including the dinner service, were added to the collection. Marla picked up the set of brass fire-irons from the sitting room.

'I'll never use these, and there's that coal scuttle as well. Somebody might like that.'

Sasha looked at her. 'What about the clothes in the boxes?'

Marla shook her head firmly. 'Somehow I think they are a clue to Uncle Andrew's life before he came here. I want to keep them a bit longer.'

Seth Yates found them looking at what they had piled up in the kitchen. He nodded briefly to Sasha, who nodded back without speaking, then he gave Marla his dazzling smile and held out a small cardboard box.

'The hens are laying well at the moment, so I thought you might like some more eggs.'

'Thank you! We finished up the last lot this morning.'

He turned to the heap on the floor. 'What's this? Are you rearranging everything?'

'We hope this is the start of the great clear-out. We're taking this to Sunday's car-boot sale.'

He looked at Marla with a frown. 'Well, be careful what you take. You don't want to sell something and then find you need it here.'

'I don't think I'll miss anything from this lot,' she said confidently.

He was still looking at the pile. 'How are you going to get it to the sale?'

'You may have noticed we have a car,' Sasha said with a touch of acid.

His lip curled. 'I saw it. I also noticed that it is very small. You won't get all this into it.'

The two girls hadn't thought of that.

'I suppose we could make two trips,' Marla said uneasily, but he was shaking his head.

'You don't want to make life difficult for yourselves so early in the morning. I'll bring my four-wheeler round, you can pile everything in it, and I'll drive you to the sale.'

'We can't expect you to do that!'

He waved Marla's protests away. 'We're neighbours. I'll be glad to help. And I'm used to getting up early, so I won't let you oversleep.'

When he had gone, Marla turned to Sasha, determined her friend should give Seth credit for his good deeds. 'Isn't he marvellous?'

'I'm not sure about that, but he certainly wants to please you.'

Marla frowned and looked at her friend in bewilderment. 'Why don't you like him, Sasha?'

Sasha hesitated, and then shrugged. 'I don't know. I suppose he's just not my type. Fortunately he's yours, so what I feel doesn't matter. Now, let's see if we can find anything else to sell.'

They unearthed a few more saleable objects, agreed on prices for most of what they were taking, and when Seth came to collect them in the half-dark Sunday morning his vehicle was soon piled high and the girls had difficulty squeezing themselves in.

'I apologise for the smell of cabbage

and the chicken mess,' he told them. 'This is a working vehicle.'

There were already plenty of cars parked and busy on the field assigned to the car-boot sale when they arrived. Seth quickly piled their stock on the grass and then drove off, promising to collect them when they called him.

Marla and Sasha set up the little table they had brought and began to arrange their more delicate items on it, only to find themselves being hampered by several men who had silently appeared from nowhere and who were intent on inspecting the goods they had to offer even before they had been unpacked properly.

'Dealers!' hissed Marla. 'They all want to get at anything valuable before somebody else finds it.'

'In that case, if they want to buy anything we double the price,' Sasha murmured.

Unfortunately, this ploy did not work for the simple reason that none of the dealers found any of their goods interesting and soon drifted away towards more promising arrivals.

The general public started to arrive about eight, and the girls got used to smiling at people who ignored their presence, examined everything carefully, made some disparaging remark, and then walked away without buying a thing. It seemed a triumph when they finally sold a china figure. Gradually the crowds grew and they sold more. Sunlight warmed them and their spirits lifted. The dinner service sold to a young couple for a reasonable price after considerable haggling. The number of china figures steadily shrank and Marla found that a very satisfactory amount was weighing down the money bag strapped to her belt.

'At least we'll be able to afford food now,' Sasha said cheerfully, 'even if we've no plates left to put it on.'

Marla was just snatching a drink of coffee from the flask they had brought with them when she was greeted by name.

'Good morning, Miss Merton.'

She scarcely recognised John Ericson in old jeans and a baggy sweater when he unexpectedly appeared before the stall. Marla welcomed him with a wide smile.

'How's it going?' he asked.

'Not too bad. Can I sell you something?'

He looked at what they had left and shook his head. 'Not unless you have some old scientific instruments, a microscope or something like that. I collect them, and it is surprising what you can sometimes find at a car-boot sale.' He moved closer to the table and spoke quietly. 'I was hoping to speak to you sometime. Can I have a word with you now?'

Leaving Sasha to guard the stall, Marla moved a short distance away with him.

'It's just that after you called the other day, I did try to find out a little more about your uncle. I discovered that he paid for the house with money from an account at a local bank which he had only opened a couple of weeks earlier. He had a small income while he was alive from an annuity which he bought at the same time as he opened the account and which ended with his death. After all this time, it would be very difficult to find out where his money was before, especially as I have no legal reason to start investigating.' He shrugged. 'Your uncle Andrew's life before he came here is a complete mystery, and I'm beginning to suspect that that is how he wanted it to be, whatever the reason.'

'And I suppose you didn't find out anything about the woman?'

'Not a thing.'

She frowned. 'Do you think he had something to hide?'

He laughed. 'It's possible. However, I doubt if he was a master criminal, if that's what you're worrying about! Perhaps he was just a very private person. In either case, I think it's best to leave things as they are rather than take the risk of stirring up something which might mean unpleasantness or even big trouble.'

Having delivered this pointed advice, he nodded farewell and turned away without waiting to see if she made any response. When she returned to the stall, scowling, Sasha cocked an enquiring eyebrow.

'What's the matter? You look as if the young solicitor has upset you.'

'Just when I think I'm getting to like him he gives another display of arrogance! He always thinks he knows best. Obviously he expects me to do as he says without daring to question his judgement. I do not like being told what to do, and if I can find a way to discover something about Uncle Andrew I will do my best to find out all I can about his life before he came to Woodham, and Mr John Ericson can't stop me!'

By mid-day the crowds were thinning as families began to drift home for Sunday lunch. Marla and Sasha had sold a satisfying quantity, but there still seemed a sizeable amount to get rid of.

'We don't want to take this lot back,' Sasha said impatiently. 'What can we do?'

'Halve the prices,' Marla said firmly.

'Are you sure?'

'Yes. A few pence is better than nothing.'

They halved the prices and then halved them again and the tactic worked. Lured by the thought of a genuine bargain, customers flocked round them, and when Seth appeared at about one o'clock he found them standing ready for him with only the table to be picked up.

'Do you mean you've sold everything?' he asked disbelievingly as they climbed into the jeep.

'We sold most of it, so then we piled everything that was left into two boxes and sold them to someone who is a regular car-boot seller.'

Marla leant back and sighed contentedly, jingling a large and heavy bag. 'I'm going to enjoy adding this lot up.'

As the girls scrambled out when they

reached Fernwood House, Seth bent down for something on the vehicle floor and then straightened up. He was holding out a bottle of wine.

'Here! I thought you might need this after all your efforts.'

Marla took it with a cry of delight, and looked at him gratefully.

'You are a true friend!'

'Enjoy it,' he laughed, and drove off.

Once indoors the two girls stripped off their coats and made a snack lunch. They had been too excited to eat breakfast and had been growing hungrier all morning, jealously eyeing the sandwiches that other more experienced car-booters had brought with them. Then they ceremonially emptied their takings out on the kitchen table, opened the wine and filled two glasses, and settled down to count the notes and coins.

Soon after they had started Sasha's mobile rang. 'Bother!' she said, trying to find out who was calling. 'The reception is hopeless in here. I'll just go outside.'

Marla nodded, intent on dividing the

coins and notes into neat piles. After some time she paused, frowning. Sasha seemed to be taking a long time over the call. Was there bad news? Just at that moment, however, Sasha burst back into the room, waving her phone triumphantly over her head.

'That was my agent,' she announced.

'Calling on a Sunday?' Marla knew how rarely agents contacted aspiring actresses out of office hours.

'There's an emergency. Howard Somers is producing a Restoration play and it's supposed to open in the West End soon, but the girl who was playing the second lead has gone missing, run away to America with her boyfriend. Somers asked my agent if he could suggest anyone who was free who could replace her at such short notice and he actually suggested me!'

It took a moment to digest this news, and then Marla hugged her friend. 'That's marvellous! So you'll be opening in the West End after all.'

But Sasha was shaking her head.

91

'Nothing's that easy. I've got to audition for him on Tuesday.' She was biting her lip. 'And my agent said that Somers insists on period plays being performed as they would have been originally — the actors have to move and behave appropriately for the time — and I haven't a clue how people behaved when Charles the Second was king.'

An idea came to Marla and a slow smile curved her lips. 'So you've got a day to learn.'

'Who's going to teach me?'

'A genuine seventeenth-century Cavalier. Remember, Seth Yates belongs to the Sealed Knot. They know everything about that period. He can help you.'

Sasha's face fell. 'He won't want the trouble. Not after the way I've treated him.'

But Marla was already looking for Seth's telephone number, and after a short call she turned triumphantly to Sasha. 'He'll be here tomorrow about eleven o'clock, dressed for the part. He says you should be wearing a full-length skirt and a top with long sleeves. Now, let's finish the wine and counting all our cash!'

It was a very satisfying total. Money worries could be forgotten for a while.

'And you won't have to dust all those horrible ornaments either,' Sasha pointed out.

Marla spent the rest of the day trying to reassure a very nervous Sasha that she would be able to grasp her big chance, and that Seth Yates could help her. She only hoped that she was speaking the truth.

★   ★   ★

Seth arrived punctually at eleven o'clock the next morning in full Cavalier dress. Marla opened the door to his knock and stood back to admire him. He swept her a bow.

'You look marvellous!' she told him. 'And it is very kind of you to help Sasha.' She lowered her voice, glancing at the kitchen door. 'This is very important to her, Seth. Chances like this don't come very often for actresses, and she's extremely nervous. No matter how she behaves, she's really very grateful to you for giving up your time to help her.'

'I'll do my best,' he promised.

Together they entered the kitchen where Sasha was lounging by the table, trying hard to appear casual and relaxed. It was not her best performance. She nodded in greeting, but did not stand.

'Sit up!' Seth barked. 'Whether you're standing or sitting, your back has to be straight.'

Scowling, Sasha pulled herself upright.

'And put your knees and feet together.'

The scowl deepened and Marla decided to run away. 'Well, I'll leave you two to get on with the lesson,' she said brightly. 'I'm going to cycle into Woodham and investigate estate agents.'

Neither of the two answered. They were too busy glowering at each other.

Marla made her escape on the old

bicycle, hoping the two would not come to blows. In town she saw an estate agent's window and stood on the pavement for some time studying the houses on offer. They all claimed to be modern or thoroughly renovated and in excellent condition. Well, Fernwood House would be a challenge to the agent's selling skills. The woman inside greeted her with a bright smile.

'Can I help you?'

'I hope so. I have a house to sell.'

'Excellent! Now if you'll just sit down I'll take the details.'

She started to write down the address of Fernwood House as Marla dictated it, but then hesitated.

'Is this that old house outside town, near Home Farm?'

'Yes.'

The woman swallowed visibly as Marla looked at her challengingly.

'Well, we'll do our best.'

Marla left ten minutes later, having arranged for an agent to come and view the property and having been given details about charges and commission. Satisfied with her morning's work, she treated herself to a coffee. By the time she had finished it more than two hours had passed since she had left Seth and Sasha, so she rode back, hoping they had managed to endure each other's company long enough for Sasha to acquire the skills she needed.

She got off the bicycle a short distance from the house and wheeled it up to the front door, anxious not to interrupt if the coaching was still in progress. She slipped into the house quietly, paused, but could hear nothing, and went through to the kitchen. Sasha should be somewhere in the house. Then, glancing casually through the window, she saw two figures outside. On the flat area at the back of the house, Seth and Sasha gravely advanced towards each other, retreated, advanced again, swept past each other and turned. Marla realised that they were performing some stately dance, silently counting out the rhythm as they created the intricate patterns. It was elegant, graceful, fascinating, and Marla held her breath and stood still, hoping a glimpse of her through the window would not disrupt their progress.

They advanced towards each other again, this time stretching out their right hands to each other. They touched, held, and suddenly the rhythm was broken, forgotten, as Seth seized Sasha in his arms and bent to kiss her. They clung to each other, Sasha responding eagerly to his embrace. Watching, Marla's eyes widened and then she hurried silently out of the front door, seized the bicycle, wheeled it away to the road, mounted it and started cycling back along the lane.

Something had happened during her time in the town, something that had turned the antagonism between Seth and Sasha into the passion that had sent them clinging to each other, oblivious to everything else. Marla laughed. Whatever it was, it had brought two people she liked together, and that had to be a good thing. She turned the bicycle back towards the house, and ensured that she made quite a bit of noise when she opened the door.

'Seth! Sasha!' she called.

Sasha appeared from the kitchen, her colour high and holding up her long skirt.

'Hallo! How did you get on with the estate agents?'

'Fine! One is calling tomorrow to see the house.' She peered past Sasha. 'How did you get on with Seth? Is he still here?'

Sasha shook her head. 'He went some time ago. He said he hoped what he'd taught me would be helpful.'

Marla frowned. Sasha was not telling the truth — or not the whole truth. Why had Seth left in such a hurry after she had seen them kissing? She decided to keep quiet about what she had witnessed until Sasha herself was ready to tell her what had happened.

'What did he teach you?'

'Oh, how to sit and stand, how to

98

walk, things like that.'

Marla waited for more details, but Sasha, who normally would have told her everything, apparently had nothing more to say this time.

'Well, it's lunchtime again. How about egg on toast?' said Marla. She could be patient and wait till her friend was ready to confide in her.

Lunch was a quiet meal. As they were finishing, Sasha pushed her plate aside and leant forward.

'Marla, you do like Seth, don't you?'

'Very much. He's kind, helpful and he's very good-looking.' She waited eagerly for Sasha to go on, but when she spoke again it had nothing to do with Seth Yates.

'Marla, I know I said I'd set off for London early tomorrow, but would you mind if I went this afternoon? Esmeralda is getting so unreliable, and I don't want to break down and be late for my audition with Howard Somers.'

'Of course you can go! Tomorrow will be an important day for you and I don't want anything to go wrong. I'll miss you, of course, and I hope you'll miss me and the people you've met here.' She stopped, still hoping that Sasha would take the hint and take her into her confidence about what had happened between her and Seth that morning, but Sasha simply gave an uncertain smile and pushed her chair back.

'I'll go and pack, then I can be well on my way before it gets dark.'

In half an hour she was ready to leave. Marla hugged her. 'I'm going to miss you, but good luck tomorrow! Call me whatever happens and tell me all about it.' She thrust a small but heavy paper bag into Sasha's hand. 'Here! This is your share of the boot sale takings.'

'But everything we sold was yours,' protested Sasha.

'It was your idea and I couldn't have done it without your help, so please take the money. I know you need it, and London is expensive.'

She did not say that Sasha would be

welcome back if she did not get the part. She did not want to even hint at the possibility of failure.

She stood waving as Esmeralda drove off noisily, and then went thoughtfully back into the house. Seth must have been too impatient, tried to go beyond a kiss and a quick embrace before Sasha had been ready, she decided, and that had scared her friend away. What a pity!

4

The house felt empty and lonely without Sasha's lively presence, but Marla sought for things to keep her busy so she did not miss her friend too much. She was up early the next morning, eager to have the house looking its best before the estate agent arrived. She tidied the kitchen, made the beds, and made sure that the stove was burning well and sending out a welcoming glow. Theo returned from his early-morning outing and curled up in his box, viewing her with apparent boredom.

'You wait!' she scolded him. 'Whoever buys this house might not like cats, and then you'll be out in the cold, looking for a new owner to spoil you.'

Theo yawned widely and went to sleep.

Ten minutes after the appointed time the estate agent had not appeared.

Marla opened the front door so that she could see if he was coming and found a man standing in the road outside, viewing the house carefully and frowning as he made notes.

'It doesn't look as if much has been done to the place for several years,' he said gloomily, having identified himself as the agent.

'It does need repainting,' Marla admitted.

'It needs more than that,' he responded, tapping the window frames with what she considered was unnecessary force.

'Come in and see its good points,' she insisted, but even inside he did not cheer up, sighing heavily as he looked in the various rooms.

'It's in a nice quiet location,' she ventured.

'It's lonely and isolated,' was the reply.

'The rooms are very convenient.'

'Small and dark.'

'It's easy to keep clean.'

A loud sniff. 'There isn't any central heating, there aren't enough electrical sockets for a modern family — in fact the whole house needs rewiring urgently. It's positively dangerous at present.'

Marla fell silent until he had finished his inspection and then faced him challengingly. 'Well?'

He shook his head. 'It's old-fashioned, neglected and badly situated. All the windows need replacing, the outside must be repointed and painted, and then the interior would have to be gutted and brought up to modern standards.'

She swallowed. 'You don't think it would fetch much?'

His smile was grim. 'Given the present state of the market, I'd say that it would be virtually impossible to sell. Even if all the work were done to it, it would still be a small, ugly, isolated house.'

Marla sank down on the nearest chair. 'So what do you suggest?'

'The best you could do is to find someone — you or somebody else

— who would live in it so it doesn't get any worse while you get essential repair work done to it when you can, and wait for the market to improve.'

'But you won't try to sell it?'

He sat down opposite her and patted her hand absent-mindedly. 'We'll put it on our books if you insist, but, to be honest, I think it would be a waste of time and your money.' He stood up and straightened his coat, obviously eager to be on his way to more profitable properties.

'Well, think about it and let us know what you decide.'

When he had gone Marla made herself a mug of coffee and sat cradling it in her hands, brooding over the situation. She knew her father would not be terribly concerned about the estate agent's verdict. He had enough money to live on in Spain and Uncle Andrew's legacy had been a pleasant unexpected stroke of luck, that was all, and he would not want his daughter to fret about it. Marla was free to lock the door of Fernwood House behind her and walk away, leaving it to slowly disintegrate or be sold for a nominal sum. The only question was, where would she go? She had no other home and no job to go to. Well, she could try and do something about that!

She reached for her mobile and settled down to call her contacts. An hour later she put the phone down, sighed heavily, and stared ahead unseeingly. It appeared no one wanted her. There seemed no question of work as an actress in the theatre and apparently few extras were wanted on the films currently being shot, nobody required her services as a model, and after the motor show nobody was yet willing to give her work that brought her in contact with the public.

Theo, purring, laid his head on her knees. Touched by this display of sympathy, Marla stroked him. 'Nobody wants me, Theo,' she said sadly.

The purring grew a little impatient, and she realised that the cat was not offering sympathy but waiting to be fed. She got up and found the last half-tin of cat food.

'Enjoy it,' she told him grimly. 'There are hard times ahead.'

She had to decide whether to stay where she was, enjoying the free accommodation, or go up to London, find somewhere dirt cheap to stay, and start knocking on doors in person in search of employment. In either case, the remainder of Uncle Andrew's bank account would come in useful and she decided to call in on John Ericson the following day to see if he could tell her exactly when she would receive it.

Her phone rang and she picked it up eagerly. Perhaps some agent, reminded of her existence, had found a job for her and was calling back. But it was Sasha.

'How did you get on at the audition?' Marla asked excitedly.

Sasha sounded uncertain. 'I think I did all right, but there wasn't much reaction from Mr Somers. There were four of us auditioning altogether and he said he'd let us know who he's selected tomorrow.' Her voice changed. 'Oh, Marla, it was so exciting to be actually standing on the stage of a West End theatre, performing in front of a famous producer! And the leading man went through a scene with each of us! I've seen him in plays and films, of course, but today I was actually speaking to him, acting with him! I do so want this part!'

'You'll get it. You deserve it. You're a marvellous actress,' Marla assured her, and Sasha gave a weak laugh.

'Thank you. The trouble is, the other girls were good as well.'

'Ring me tomorrow and let me know the verdict,' Marla instructed her. 'I'll stand by to congratulate you.'

The next morning when Marla entered the solicitors' office Beryl looked up eagerly, a smile of welcome forming, but it disappeared as she looked past Marla and realised that she was alone.

'Oh! Your friend isn't with you? She said she would have something for me.'

Marla remembered the signed photograph of the television actor and regretfully shook her head. 'She had to go back to London suddenly.'

Beryl's shoulders sagged. 'Oh well, it doesn't matter. I suppose she could have given it to you, though.'

Marla decided a little white lie would be forgivable. 'She asked me to tell you that she was still looking for the photo, but really it was difficult for her to think of anything else except getting up to London. She has been offered an audition with Howard Somers for a part in a play that's opening soon in the West End!'

Beryl forgot her own concerns and listened eagerly as Marla explained the situation. She was obviously fascinated by this fresh news from the acting world.

'And she'll hear today if she's got the part?'

'Yes, and I'll make sure to ask her about the photograph when she calls.'

'Oh, don't bother about that. This is much more exciting! Do let me know what happens!' She seemed to recall her duties. 'I suppose you want to see Mr Ericson?'

'If it's possible.'

Marla looked at John's door, but it was shut and she could hear no signs of activity.

'I'm afraid he's had to go out to see someone, but he should be back soon. His father is here, but he's semi-retired and I don't think he knows anything about your affairs. Would you like to wait and have a coffee?'

Marla accepted the offer and as the two women chatted she learned that Beryl was a keen member of the local amateur dramatic society.

'When I was young I actually dreamed of being an actress,' the secretary confessed wistfully, 'but I had to earn a living so I ended up in an office. I am jealous of you and Sasha.'

'Don't be jealous of me,' Marla said emphatically. 'I had big dreams as well, but I have had to realise recently that they're not going to come true, and I just don't know what I'm going to do next.'

'So you've nothing planned, nothing that will take you away from Woodham soon?'

'No, but I'll have to start earning some money soon. Have you any suggestions?'

Beryl Richards looked pensive, and at that moment the door opened to admit John Ericson. He looked pleased to see Marla and she smiled at him warmly. In spite of what she thought of as his arrogance, her anger over their last encounter faded as she appreciated the help he had given her. He was a young, intelligent and attractive man, and she appreciated that he had done more to help her than was strictly required of him; she was beginning to see him as a possible friend as well as a solicitor. She felt even better when, in his office, he told her that four hundred pounds was being transferred to her bank account that week.

'That will be very useful, whether I

go to London or not,' she told him.

He frowned. 'You're still thinking of leaving, of going back to London?'

'I need a job,' she said bluntly, 'though after the way I left my last one it may be difficult to find anybody who'll employ me.' She told him about the incident at the motor show and he laughed.

'It sounds to me as if you did the right thing. I'm sure my mother would agree, and there's a friend of hers . . . ' He hesitated, suddenly thoughtful. 'I wonder. I think I may be able to help you. There may be a job — at least for a time — in Woodham, if you don't mind staying here for a while longer. Just give me your mobile number so I can get in touch with you if I have any luck. I can't promise anything, but I'll do my best.'

Marla left his office feeling happier than she had done since the estate agent's visit. She smiled and said goodbye to Beryl, but just as she was about to open the outer door her phone rang. She slipped it out of her bag, put it to her ear and then hastily moved it away as she was greeted with an ear-splitting scream. The voice that followed was Sasha's.

'I've got the part! We open in two weeks. I'm not going to have time to sleep, what with learning my lines and rehearsing.'

'Congratulations! I knew you would get it!'

'Well I didn't!'

Marla saw that Beryl was staring at her, wildly guessing at the conversation.

'She's got it!' she hissed, and the secretary squealed with delight.

'I'm so pleased!' she exclaimed. 'Tell her so.'

'Tell her yourself!' and she passed the phone to the eager receptionist, who added her good wishes to Marla's and then listened to Sasha with laughter and evident delight before passing the phone back

'So it's congratulations from Beryl as well as from me,' Marla said.

'Thank you both. I've got to go now,' Sasha gabbled, 'but I'll call again as soon as I have time so I can tell you more.' She paused. 'Incidentally, thank Seth Yates when you see him. Apparently what I learnt from him helped me look right and that was important in landing the part.'

Beryl was greedy for more information which Marla couldn't give her. 'When I hear from her again I'll call in and bring you up to date,' she promised.

She was conscious of very mixed feelings as she made her way home. She was delighted for Sasha, of course she was, but there was a touch of envy as well. Sasha was achieving what she herself had hoped for a few years ago. Now it seemed as if her immediate future was being decided for her. If John could find her an employer in Woodham, then of course she would have to stay at Fernwood House. She had no other viable option.

Seth Yates was at the gate of Home

Farm. She waved to him and stopped her bicycle. He looked at the plastic bag of shopping dangling from one of the handlebars.

'You don't have to keep riding into town on that antique bike. If you want to do some proper shopping, let me know and I'll run you in,' he offered.

'Thank you. I may take you up on that, as I've just heard that Sasha has got the part in the play, so she and Esmeralda won't be coming back for some time.'

He looked politely pleased, no more. 'She must be delighted. Give her my congratulations and best wishes.'

'She is! And she specially asked me to thank you. She said her success was largely due to the tuition in seventeenth-century manners that you gave her.'

'Glad to be of help.' His smile reappeared. 'Remember, I'm available as a taxi service as well as a drama coach, and all I ask in return is a cup of tea.'

'As I said, I may need your help if I stay.' She told him about the estate agent.

'So I may just go back to London, or I may try for work round here.'

'Stay,' he said urgently.

She looked at him in surprise and he gave a crooked smile. 'If you leave, the house will decay and lose what value it has, and I'm not very happy about having an empty house near me anyway. You never know who might move in and try to take it over or hide there.'

Marla felt her spirits rise as she rode the last short stretch back to her temporary home. Seth Yates definitely still wanted her to stay, and that was flattering, whatever the reason. However, although she liked him, that was all. She did not find him as attractive as John Ericson's slow smile and blond good looks, and she hoped the young solicitor would call her soon.

But instead of calling, he arrived on her doorstep the following morning. 'I had to come this way because I've got an appointment in the next village,' he explained, following her into the house. He halted and looked round the kitchen appreciatively. 'You've done a lot of work. This looks much better.'

'But not good enough to sell,' she sighed. 'Have you got time for a cup of tea?'

'Yes, please.' He watched her put the kettle on. 'I'm here because I told my mother about your problems and she contacted an old friend, and the result is that there is the possibility of a job.' Marla swung round, eyes sparkling, but he shook his head. 'Don't get too excited. It may not interest you. It's something to do with council houses.' He dug out a small piece of paper and handed it to her. 'If you call this lady, Miss Charter, she'll be able to tell you what it involves.'

'Does she know about my past?'

'Miss Charter has a low opinion of men. She scares me. If she knew that you slapped a man for taking liberties she would probably give you the job, sight unseen.'

They were laughing together when there was another knock at the door.

117

Seth Yates stood outside. 'I brought you some more eggs,' he said, holding out a bag.

'Oh, thank you. Your fresh eggs taste much better than the shop-bought ones.'

She thought that was all, but instead of leaving he stood there, obviously waiting to be invited in.

'My solicitor, John Ericson, is here,' she said brightly.

'I saw his car.' He did not move, and she could scarcely shut the door in his face.

'Would you like to come in for a cup of tea?' she asked resignedly.

In the kitchen, the two young men greeted each other warily.

'Of course, you two must know each other,' Marla commented.

'All our lives,' said John Ericson. 'We were at school together. We've been rivals in the playground, on the sports field, and in other matters since we were six.'

'Who won most often?'

'Oh, I think we're about equal,' said Seth. 'Neither of us likes being beaten.'

The two seemed to be drinking their tea with deliberate slowness, as if each was determined to outstay the other, till Marla lost her patience.

'Well, if you will excuse me,' she said, standing up, 'I have a lot of work to see to.'

Obediently they put down their cups and left, though John managed to linger for a few final seconds.

'Let me know how you get on with Miss Charter,' he murmured before following Seth.

It might be flattering to have two young men competing for her attention, but it was also time-wasting, and Marla gave a sigh of relief as she shut the front door and returned to the kitchen. She picked up the piece of paper. What did she know about council houses? Still, it was worth following up, and she called the number.

'Charter here,' said a crisp female voice.

'Er — my name's Marla Merton, and John Ericson said you had a vacancy

— something to do with council housing.'

'Oh, you're the girl who's living in that god-forsaken house out in the wilds — Fernwood House. John's mother told me about you. Yes, we do need someone urgently. If you'll come and see me, I'll explain what the job involves and we can see if you're suitable.' There was a rustle of paper. 'How about this afternoon? Three o'clock?'

Another ride into town! But it had to be done and Marla assured Miss Charter that she would be at the address she gave her at three o'clock.

'Good. And be on time.'

The call ended and Marla was left to plan as best she could for the coming meeting. She was accustomed to interviews and auditions, but this job would be quite unlike any of the others she had applied for in the past. How should she present herself? Miss Charter was clearly a no-nonsense lady, not likely to be impressed by looks, and she might disapprove of attention-seeking clothes and make-up. Marla told herself she had to think as if she were auditioning for a part as a council worker. The trouble was, she didn't think she'd ever encountered one and had no idea what they were like.

When she set off that afternoon, in good time for the appointment, she was wearing a plain jacket and skirt, and flat shoes. Her hair was pulled back from her face, and she wore no make-up apart from a little lipstick. Looking in the mirror, she had told herself that she looked eminently respectable, not at all like an aspiring actress and model.

At the council offices she asked for Miss Charter.

'Is she expecting you?'

'Yes.'

She had the impression that the receptionist gave her a look of sympathy as she gave her directions to Miss Charter's office.

Soon she found herself in the presence of Miss Charter, an impressively large lady in a strictly tailored suit with heavy dark-framed glasses, who greeted her briefly and then instructed her to sit. This was followed by an unnerving silence as Miss Charter inspected Marla for some time. Marla began to fidget uneasily.

'I understand that you have never worked in an office before,' Miss Charter said. 'What have you done?'

Marla had prepared a description of her past experience with details of some employment. She handed this over and it was scrutinised carefully, Miss Charter's eyebrows rising from time to time.

'Very interesting,' she said finally. 'Well, we have this vacancy because the woman who was doing the work became pregnant and the baby arrived prematurely, so we've been left with no one to cover her job three weeks earlier than we expected. It's not a permanent job, by the way, just till she can come back from maternity leave.'

Now the interview proper began. Miss Charter explained that the job entailed dealing with the maintenance of council properties. If a tenant discovered a leak, for example, they would telephone or call in the offices, report the fault, and the official would arrange for a plumber to call.

'Basically it should be straightforward,' Miss Charter insisted. 'The trouble is that some people expect instant miracles and won't accept that the fault can't be put right within the hour, and sometimes they are trying to get the property improved rather than repaired. How are you when people get really irritating?'

Marla remembered the motor show. 'I try and stay calm and polite,' she responded, 'but sometimes you have to make it clear that people have gone too far and you are not prepared to put up with it.'

This got an approving nod. 'Good. We don't want someone who'll promise a tenant everything they want just to get rid of them. And what use, Miss Merton, do you think your acting experience would be in this post?'

This was the difficult question! Marla looked Miss Charter straight in the eye and gave the answer she had spent some time devising. 'It means I can adapt my behaviour to suit different situations and people.'

A smile finally dawned on Miss Charter's stern face. 'A good answer! Well, Miss Merton, we do need someone as quickly as possible, especially as winter is now setting in and bad weather always brings problems. I sometimes wonder what people do to their houses over Christmas. Would you accept the post, starting on Monday? Of course, you understand that if you do not prove suitable you will have to leave.'

Marla, surprised and delighted, said she quite understood and was eager to start. Salary and various other matters were explained to her. Finally she was ready to leave and Miss Charter shook hands with her.

'I look forward to working with you,' she announced. 'You seem a very sensible young woman.' Then she bit her lip. 'There is one thing. You do look a little forbidding. May I suggest a little more make-up to soften your image, to make you more approachable?'

Marla promised to try this, laughing inwardly as she thought of the extensive collection of cosmetics she had to choose from, and then she climbed on her bike and rode back along the country lanes, singing happily.

She had a home, a job and a bank balance!

By Monday morning, however, she was a nervous wreck, conscious that she was launching herself into a completely unknown world. She cycled into Woodham with her heart thumping and a feeling that she was making a great mistake. At one point she halted. Should she turn round, go back, and call Miss Charter to say she had changed her mind? But that would be cowardly, and she did need the job, or at least the money it would bring her. She rode on and arrived very early, which meant she had to wait outside the council building for Miss

Charter to appear. That lady greeted her with a brisk nod.

'Good! Punctuality is important.'

Then she was shown into a small room near the main entrance. It had a desk with a telephone on it facing the door, two chairs and a filing cabinet. Behind the desk was another door which led into an inner corridor. 'Your escape route,' said Miss Charter.

She was given a list of telephone numbers as well as a great pile of forms. Some apparently needed action while others had to be filed. Miss Charter spent some time explaining things to her. 'Remember,' Miss Charter said sternly, 'it is very important that all forms are properly filled in and neatly filed. Now I'll leave you to get on with it. If you need help, call me.'

Left on her own, Marla spent the first hour inspecting the drawers of the desk (empty, except for some old paper-clips) and trying to master which form related to which emergency. When the phone rang she grabbed it, dropped it, rescued it, and managed a shaky, 'Hello?'

A very agitated woman's voice informed her that a pipe had burst and water was leaking all over the kitchen floor. Marla took the name, address and telephone number and promised that action would be taken. Then she found the plumber's telephone number on her list, contacted him, and was assured he would see to the matter that morning. She called the woman back to give her the good news, filled in the appropriate form, and began to relax a little.

Later there was another call, this time about some shaky banisters, which the caller did admit might be due to her son's recent delight in sliding down them. Marla arranged for a carpenter to call.

Maybe this job wouldn't be too difficult after all.

Then came a loud knock on the door, which was flung open before she had time to respond. A large and very belligerent man stormed in and slammed his hand on her desk.

'I've told you lot before that that jerry-built death-trap you've put my family in isn't fit to live in. Now the toilet's broken! I demand to be rehoused!' He glared at her. 'Do something!'

Flustered, Marla reached for a pen and some paper. 'Can I have your name and address, please?'

'Ted Barker. And you shouldn't need to be told. I've been in here so often that I should think everybody knows my name and what a terrible place I live in.' He leant across the desk aggressively. 'I want a four-bedroom house on that new estate, and if I don't get it soon, you're in trouble!'

Marla faced him, wondering how to tackle the situation. She remembered what she had said to Miss Charter. She would not be Marla Merton, scared novice; instead she would assume the part of a cool, calm and experienced professional who did not frighten easily. She stood up and looked coldly at the man glowering at her.

'Mr Barker, I am here to deal with

problems of maintenance. Give me your address and I will send someone to see to the problem with the toilet. If you want anything else, you will have to contact the relevant officer.'

She thought she sounded very pompous, but it was obvious that Barker had thought that he could easily intimidate a young woman and her apparent composure baffled him. He started to shout about the poor condition of his house and Marla waited till he stopped and then, once again, asked for his address. Finally he gave it to her and left, slamming the door behind him.

As soon as he left the door behind her opened and Miss Charter appeared. She was actually giggling.

'You handled that very well,' she said approvingly.

'Were you listening to what happened?'

'Oh, yes. I saw our Mister Barker coming in, and I listened at the door to see how you would cope. I would have come in if you needed help. But you didn't! You managed him perfectly.'

'Does he often come here then?'

'Frequently. He was one of the reasons one girl left. He wants a new, four-bedroom house and he's not entitled to one, so he's hoping to wear us down by complaining as often as possible.' She patted Marla on the shoulder. 'You've started well. Now run along to the canteen and have a cup of tea.'

There were no more major incidents and Marla went home at the end of the day tired out but triumphant. She had survived.

By the end of the week she was settled in and feeling reasonably competent. She was really pleased when she could get hot water restored to a family with a young baby, or make an old lady feel safer by getting her front-door lock mended. It helped when a couple of tenants took the trouble to call back and thank her for her assistance. In between calls she filled in forms and mastered the filing system.

Seth called at Fernwood House a

couple of times during the week with the excuse of small gifts of eggs or vegetables, and was obviously pleased by the way she had settled into her job.

'You'll be here for the next forty years,' he told her.

She shook her head. 'Not unless I can afford to get the windows fixed in this house. I am afraid they are going to fall out when the wind blows, they rattle so loudly.'

'Well, I'm sure someone will be willing to give you a home if that happens,' he said meaningfully.

She hastily changed the subject. 'Sasha's been calling me every evening. Sometimes she's happy as anything because she feels she is really doing well, and then Somers criticises the way she does a scene and she's sure she is going to be a complete disaster and ruin the play.' Marla laughed. 'This is the first Restoration comedy she has appeared in, and she is quite surprised by how rude some of it is.'

'When does it open?'

'In five days' time. I shall read all the reviews.'

'Let me know what they say,' he said politely but with apparent indifference.

Sometimes she found it difficult to believe that she had seen him passionately embracing Sasha. She wished she had told her friend that she had observed them and so forced Sasha to confide in her.

The day of the play's opening arrived. Marla called Sasha early and wished her luck.

'I'll need it,' Sasha said pitifully. 'I'm sitting here, shivering with stage fright.'

'You've got a good play, a marvellous cast, and a great director.'

Sasha managed a laugh. 'And I have learnt my lines. I'll call you as soon as I can.'

5

That evening Marla's eyes constantly went to the clock. At the hour when she knew the curtain would rise she imagined Sasha standing in the wings, waiting for her first entrance, her first speech. Mentally she wished her good luck. When it was time for the play to end, she could visualise the actors lined up against the final curtain, acknowledging the applause. Would their reception be half-hearted, members of the public fumbling for their bags instead of clapping; or would it be rapturous, a standing ovation? She sat waiting for Sasha's call. Time passed, and her phone was silent. Did that mean the evening had been a disaster and Sasha could not bring herself to tell Marla the bad news? Finally she gave up and went to bed late, afraid her friend's hopes and ambitions had been once again frustrated.

The next morning she left for work early, called in at the newsagent's, and bought a copy of every national newspaper on display. The shopkeeper could not suppress his curiosity.

'You've got a lot of reading there,' he observed.

Marla nodded. 'I'm conducting a survey on the press's reaction to a certain item of news,' she replied, and he looked suitably impressed.

The floor of her office was soon covered with discarded sheets of newsprint as she rejected sports supplements and news pages in her hunt for play reviews. When she had found about a dozen she began to read the top one. Her eyes widened. She threw it aside and went on to the next, written by a distinguished theatre critic. She read it, reread it, then settled down in her chair and slowly worked through the rest. When she had finished, tears were running down her face, but they were tears of happiness. The play was a triumph! Every critic lauded it, praising the direction, acting, costumes — every aspect of the production. And in every review, as well as praise being showered on the leading actors, Sasha was singled out for special mention as well. Her ability was recognised and there was speculation about her future. Sasha was a success, finally on her way to becoming a star!

Marla found that she was dancing round her office, her hands clasped above her head in triumph. Clients that morning found themselves greeted by a wide, sunny smile and left feeling that Marla positively welcomed the chance to solve their problems.

The call she was waiting for finally came at midday. Sasha was full of apologies.

'I didn't get to bed till early this morning, and I've just woken up. I'm sorry I didn't call last night, but there just wasn't a chance. All through the performance we knew that it was going well. You could feel the audience's response, and at the end they were standing and applauding, cheering and whistling. I was in tears! I just couldn't help it! Afterwards there was a party and we stayed up for the papers. Have you read them?'

'Every one,' Marla said happily. 'Your dreams are coming true at last, Sasha.'

There was silence for a while.

'I think so,' Sasha said tremulously. 'I hope so.'

'They are! Now have a rest and get ready for tonight. Remember, you've got to give a great performance every night.'

She had just ended the call when there was a knock on the door. It was time to return to the real world.

'Come in!' she said, and was very surprised when John Ericson put his head round the door.

'What are you doing here?' she demanded. 'You haven't got a council house.'

'No, but I had to see Miss Charter and she asked me to give you these.' He put a sheaf of forms on her desk. 'I am also running away from a stage-struck secretary,' he sighed, sitting down on the chair opposite her. He nodded at the collection of newspapers she had piled up in a corner. 'Beryl has got nearly as many as you, and she hasn't got much work done this morning because she keeps rereading the reviews of your friend's play and reading out the good bits to me.'

'Isn't it wonderful!' Marla marvelled. 'I always knew Sasha would do well if she was given the chance.'

He looked at her thoughtfully from under his long eyelashes. 'Do you wish the same thing had happened to you?' he asked quietly.

Her smile was a little wistful. 'I had to admit years ago that I hadn't got enough talent for the stage.' She sat up briskly. 'Now, is there anything I can do for you?'

'The visit to Miss Charter was an excuse. I could have phoned her. I'm actually here on behalf of my mother.

She knows Miss Charter can be a little difficult and she's feeling somewhat guilty about suggesting you work for her, so I've been sent to see how you are surviving.'

'Oh, you can tell her that Miss Charter and I are getting on well so far. There's no need for her to worry.'

'Good. Then perhaps you'd like to tell her that in person and celebrate your success at the same time. She would like you to come to dinner with us tomorrow.'

His mother might want to see her, but how did he feel about her being invited into his home? There had been no particular enthusiasm in his voice. Marla considered for a moment and came up with an excuse.

'I'd love to,' she said, 'but you know I live rather a long way out of town and I don't know where you live or how far away it is. I don't fancy a long bike ride in the dark.'

'Don't worry. I certainly don't expect you to cycle to our house and then back again along those lonely lanes. I'll pick you up at seven o'clock, if that's all right, and take you home again afterwards.'

She smiled politely, unable to think of another excuse. 'That would solve my problems. Thank your mother very much. I'd love to come.'

'I'll see you tomorrow, then. Good-bye.'

He was gone, leaving Marla to neglect her filing for a while as she fretted about what she should wear for her first social engagement in Woodham, an evening with an elderly solicitor and his wife. John Ericson had seen her tired and pale after a long journey, windblown after a bike ride, and wrapped in an apron as she saw to the house, so she couldn't impress him. After considerable thought, she settled on a plain black wool dress. A gold chain necklace and bracelet would make it dressy enough for the evening.

John Ericson gave her a long approving look when he arrived to collect her the following evening.

'The right image?' she asked nervously.

He nodded. 'You look good. Of course my parents may be hoping for something a little more outrageous, as they know you used to be an actress.'

Her face fell. 'Should I change? Add a bit more bling?'

He laughed and held the door open. 'I like you as you are, and so will they.'

As she had expected, the Ericsons lived in a large detached house on the outskirts of Woodham in what was obviously a very select area. John turned into the wide paved drive, and the front door opened as he switched the engine of his car off. He nodded at the figure in the doorway. 'Mother has been listening out for our arrival.'

Marla had been feeling nervous, but Mrs Ericson was as blonde as her son, with big, mischievous blue eyes and a curvy, comfortable figure. She took Marla's hands in hers. 'Come in, dear, and please tell me you like working with Miss Charter or I'm going to have a miserable evening.'

Marla giggled and relaxed, and was led in to meet Mr Ericson, an older, white-haired version of John. Drinks were produced and she was installed in a comfortable chair as they sat round a blazing open fire. She had wondered what they would talk about, but soon found that was no problem. They wanted to know what she thought of Woodham, of Miss Charter, of her job, of Fernwood House and, somewhat surprisingly, of Seth Yates.

'The Sealed Knot is active in this area,' commented Mr Ericson. 'I've often seen several members riding along looking magnificent in their uniforms.'

'I'm surprised he's still single,' added Mrs Ericson. 'He does look glamorous all dressed up, and he's got a very good farm. I know his mother would like to see him married.'

'Perhaps he's too busy with his hobby and his farm to go courting,' said her husband.

John was noticeably silent.

The meal was simple, traditional English

food well cooked and served. Marla thoroughly enjoyed it, and happily accepted a second helping of the apple pudding. 'It is a long time since I've had a meal like this,' she apologised. 'On my own I tend to settle for snacks, and even when Sasha was here we didn't spend much time cooking.'

'Sasha!' John exclaimed. 'I knew there was something I had to tell you. Beryl is taking next Friday off. She didn't ask me whether she could go, she told me! She and a friend have got tickets for Sasha's play and they are going to London for the weekend to see it next Saturday. She borrowed a copy from the library and I think she's enjoyed being mildly shocked by it.'

'Does that explain all the giggles in the office?' his father asked. 'I wondered what was the matter.'

It was a pleasant evening. The conversation covered a wide field. Mrs Ericson told Marla about a couple of societies which she thought might interest her, and Marla began to feel that for the first time in her life she was being accepted as a member of a community. Of course, she would only be a temporary member. As soon as the house sold she would be going back to London, but she did not say this. She did not want them to know that she saw their pleasant little town as second-best, somewhere to stay only till she got a chance for something better.

She learned that John Ericson lived in a self-contained annexe to the house.

'It's what is usually called a 'granny flat',' explained Mrs Ericson. 'He does live an independent life and gets most of his own meals, though I am graciously permitted to do his washing and ironing!'

Then Marla saw Mr Ericson stifle a yawn, and when she looked stealthily at her watch she realised that it was getting late. She thanked her hosts sincerely for a most enjoyable evening and John drove her home. He saw her to the door and waited till she had opened it. She turned to say goodbye, but he shook his head.

'If you don't mind, I'd like to stay until you've made sure that the house is safe, that nobody has broken in.'

She halted, taken aback and giving a fearful glance at the dark interior of the house. 'Do you think that's likely?'

'It's possible,' he said rather grimly. 'There have been incidents of isolated houses in the area being burgled recently.'

Fortunately, a quick check showed that Fernwood House had not suffered from intruders.

'Well, thank your parents again for the evening, and thank you for the lifts,' Marla said.

He smiled down at her, laid his hands gently on her shoulders, and drew her close. She realised he was about to kiss her and her body tensed. She had enjoyed seeing a more relaxed and pleasant side of him that evening and was ready, almost eager, to receive his kiss, but at the same time she was aware how vulnerable she was, alone with him in this isolated house. He must have sensed this, for he kissed the top of her head gently and then released her abruptly.

'Thank you for your company,' he said softly. 'Sleep well.'

Then he was gone, leaving her half relieved and half regretful. He had his faults, but he was an honourable man.

It was clear the next morning that Seth Yates had a much lower opinion of him. He appeared early while she was still sleepy from the unaccustomed late night out. 'Did you enjoy your evening out with Ericson?' he asked, handing her yet another half dozen eggs. 'I noticed you didn't encourage him to stay very long when he brought you back.'

Marla glared at him indignantly. 'Were you spying on me?' she demanded, and thrust the eggs back into his hands. 'Here, take these. I don't want them if they are just an excuse to come prying. My life is my own, and what I do with it has nothing to do with you.'

Seth turned red. 'I'm sorry. I apologise. There is a very narrow line between being a neighbour looking out for a young woman living on her own and appearing too nosy and — honestly — I just like to check that you are safe.'

'I can look after myself,' Marla insisted.

He apologised again. 'I'm sorry, but you won't have to worry about me spying on you next weekend. I came to tell you that I will be away for four days. My parents will be coming over to keep an eye on things, so you may see them, or they may call in.'

Before he left she graciously let him persuade her to accept the eggs.

The next day she went shopping in Woodham and called in at the Ericsons' office, her excuse being to ask John to pass on her thanks for a very pleasant evening. He was out, but the visit was not wasted because she was able to achieve her other aim, to ask Beryl Richards about her visit to London to see Sasha on stage. Beryl was obviously excited at the prospect. She was going to London with another member of the amateur dramatic society.

'This is the first time I'll have known one of the actors in a professional production I've seen,' she said proudly.

Marla told her how much she wished she could go with her, and managed to learn the details of which performance and which seats Beryl had booked. Marla passed on this information the next time Sasha called.

'Are you getting used to success?' she enquired.

There was a laugh. 'I'll never get used to it, but I have got more confidence. I've stopped feeling that it is a fluke whenever the audience applauds me — and I do love that sound.' Sasha sighed. 'Of course, it's only a short run because of the leading man's film commitments, but it has stirred up interest in me. I am getting enquiries from various places and my agent says she's got a long list of future options for me to consider.' She paused. 'Anything interesting happening in Woodham?'

Marla told her about the dinner with

the Ericsons. 'It was very pleasant. They're a nice family.'

'Especially the son?'

Marla was still not sure exactly what she thought of John Ericson and she was not prepared to debate her feelings over the telephone. 'He's all right. But Seth Yates was very jealous the next morning. I was very flattered. I didn't realise he cared so much.'

She waited to see how Sasha responded to this provocative remark, but her friend made no comment.

Later that week, on her way back after the day's work, Marla saw a smart saloon car parked outside Home Farm instead of the usual ancient jeep. She decided it must belong to Seth's parents, and the next morning, Saturday, she called round to introduce herself. A comfortable-looking woman in her late fifties opened the door in response to her knock, and greeted her warmly after she had introduced herself.

'Marla Merton! Seth has told us all about you. Come in! My husband's out doing something on the farm at the moment but I was just about to make myself a fresh pot of tea.'

This was the first time Marla had been inside Home Farm and she looked around with interest as she was led into a large kitchen. An Aga kept the room warm, rows of copper saucepans hung on the low beams, and the centre was dominated by a large scrubbed-wood table. In spite of the size of the kitchen, the impression was cosy and welcoming. Mrs Yates laughed as she saw Marla inspecting everything.

'It doesn't look like a bachelor's home, does it? I liked it like this, but I thought that when we moved out Seth would have it refitted in a more modern style. But apparently he's as fond of this look as I was.' She produced a plate of scones fresh from the oven as well as a pot of tea and settled down, obviously ready for a long chat. 'Seth told us how you were an actress and a model before you came here to sell Fernwood House, but that now you seem to be settling in nicely and you've even got a job in town. Are you still trying to sell the house?'

'It is for sale, but nobody has shown the slightest interest, so I don't know how long I will be staying here — a few months or as long as a year. But at the moment life here suits me very well. I understand you made a big change as well — from the farm to a house in town. How are you enjoying that?'

'Very much. We loved having the farm, but we had reached an age when we hadn't got the energy we used to have and the work was becoming a burden. Now I can be shopping in the centre of town in ten minutes, or we can jump into the car and be in the country in no time. It is a new life. I'm still getting used to floors without mud on them.'

'I suppose Seth finds running the farm by himself a bit demanding.'

'It is a full-time job, but he can hire help when he needs it, and George and I are always willing to lend a hand. He wouldn't have been able to go to London this week if we weren't able to move in.'

Marla's eyes widened in surprise. 'London? He didn't say where he was going.'

Mrs Yates frowned. 'I'm not sure why he's going there. He muttered something about business matters, but didn't say any more.' Her voice grew confidential. 'I didn't ask him too much because, personally, I hope he's gone to see some girlfriend. It's time he got married. A farmer needs a wife and I'd like some grandchildren while I can enjoy them.'

Her voice was full of meaning and Marla remembered what the Ericsons had said about Mrs Yates' wish for a daughter-in-law. She wondered whether she was expected to declare an interest in the post of farmer's wife, and sought for a way of changing the subject. She looked up at the dark roof beams.

'This looks much older than Fernwood House.'

Mrs Yates nodded emphatically. 'It's been altered over time, of course, but basically it dates from the time of Queen Elizabeth.'

'That old! It may be much older but it looks in better condition than Fernwood House. I'm afraid Uncle Andrew neglected his home.' She turned to Mrs Yates. 'You lived next to him for some years. Did you get to know him?'

Mrs Yates shrugged. 'We tried to be good neighbours, but he made it clear that he didn't want anything much to do with us. At first I thought he might be shy, so I used to take him a few eggs and try to chat, but he never even asked me in. Nobody ever visited him and I don't think he even got many letters.'

'He seems to have been a mystery man,' commented Marla. 'Even his own family didn't know where he was or what he was doing for several years before my father heard from the lawyers that he had died.'

'Some people just like to be on their own and hate getting involved with other people.' Mrs Yates started to clear away the tea things. 'It was a pity, because I always had an interest in Fernwood House. You know there used to be a much bigger, grander house there which was destroyed in the Civil War?'

Marla nodded. 'Seth told me that.'

'Did he tell you that the house was named after the family that owned it and the estate around it? The Fernwoods were rich and powerful at one time. Well, my maiden name was Fernwood. Seth spent a long time tracing our family tree and he's convinced that I am a descendant of that family. I think that's one reason why he's so interested in playing Cavaliers and Roundheads with the Sealed Knot.'

'So you're an aristocrat?'

Mrs Yates bubbled with laughter. 'No! The money and power went hundreds of years ago, and if I have any noble blood, it's only a few drops and the rest is very common. I'm a farmer's wife.'

Marla had a sudden vision of Seth as

a rather lonely little boy on an isolated farm, dreaming of his splendid ancestors, wishing he could be like them. When he was dressed as a Cavalier and looked in the mirror, did he see Seth Yates or one of those noble ancestors?

★   ★   ★

A couple of days later, during her lunch break, she called in the solicitors' office, curious to hear what Beryl Richards had thought of Sasha and the play. The receptionist greeted her eagerly.

'I was going to call you, to see if we could meet so that I could tell you all about it!'

'Was it good?'

The receptionist clasped her hands together and rolled her eyes. 'It was marvellous! I don't think I've ever seen such a superb production! And the acting!'

'Sasha was good?'

Beryl Richards nodded enthusiastically. 'She is going to be a great actress!'

she beamed. 'But that wasn't all. During the interval the usher came round asking for Miss Beryl Richards. I told him that was me, and he said that Sasha wanted my friend and me to go round backstage when the performance was over! We couldn't believe it!' Her eyes were shining.

'You went, of course.'

'Of course. Sasha welcomed us as if we were both old friends and introduced us to all the actors.' She looked smug. 'Mary was very impressed by the way Sasha treated us.'

Marla remembered the post-performance gatherings of her own limited acting career, and felt a distinct pang of nostalgia, but she controlled it. 'Well, I'm glad you thought it worth the trip to London. I don't suppose many people from Woodham will see the play.'

'Oh, but there was at least one other. That young man who lives near you — Seth Yates. He was there. I don't think he saw us, however, and clearly he hadn't been invited backstage.'

This was very interesting news, but frustrating because Beryl hadn't spoken to Seth and did not think he would have recognised her. The evening at the theatre was obviously going to be one of the great events of Beryl's year and she chatted on happily for some time, glad of a listener who could appreciate what had happened.

She did invite Marla to join the local dramatic society, saying they would obviously benefit from her experience, but Marla managed to reject this invitation, pointing out that she did not know how long she would be in Woodham, and didn't want to leave them in the lurch by deserting them in the middle of a production. Marla finally escaped after promising to pass on any more news from Sasha.

A few days later Seth appeared with some fresh leeks and potatoes. They chatted for a while and Marla mentioned her meeting with his mother, though apparently he had already heard about it.

'Mother enjoyed meeting you. In fact she said she'd like to see you again sometime.' But he did not volunteer any information about what he had been doing during his absence. Finally, tired of waiting for him to bring up the subject, Marla decided to ask him directly.

'Did you enjoy your visit to London?'

'It was a business visit — rather boring.'

Marla went on the attack. 'But it wasn't all business, was it? Beryl Richards saw you at the theatre. Did you enjoy it? What did you think of Sasha?'

He was frowning, as though angry that his presence had been seen and talked about. 'I had an evening to fill, so I decided I might as well go and see the play. It was all right, though I don't know much about Restoration comedies, so I probably missed a lot of the jokes.'

'And Sasha?'

'She was quite good.'

He seemed reluctant to add anything else and went soon afterwards, leaving

Marla to wonder how he had managed to get a ticket at the last minute for a play which had been sold out for the rest of the run.

Day followed day without anything happening to break the routine. Marla coped with most of her clients without any trouble, occasionally referring to Miss Charter if she had an unusually awkward customer, but this was rare. She could even deal with Ted Barker without too much upset. She got to know some of the other council workers and benefited from their advice on which were the best shops for bargains.

However, sitting in an office for most of the day left her short of exercise, and one sunny autumn evening she set out for a walk along the lane. About a mile from Fernwood House she saw a car parked by the side of the road. It looked vaguely familiar, and as she got closer she saw that it was John Ericson's car. He was standing near it, gazing over the fields through a pair of binoculars, and did not hear her approach.

'Good evening,' she said loudly.

He jumped, dropped the binoculars, and she heard him swear softly as he bent to collect them from an inconvenient patch of nettles.

'I'm sorry,' she said repentantly, 'I didn't mean to startle you.'

'And you must excuse my language.' He was wiping the binoculars clean.

'What are you looking at?' she said with curiosity. As far as she could see there was nothing particularly interesting in the nearby fields.

'I was bird-watching,' he told her. 'I'm pretty sure I saw a buzzard. They have been seen near here.'

To Marla a buzzard sounded like something from a western film, a bird of prey that might attack anything that moved. 'A buzzard! Aren't they dangerous? Do they attack people?'

He laughed, shaking his head. 'Only small animals, not you.'

She lingered, intrigued by his interest. 'Are you a keen bird-watcher?'

He nodded as he put the binoculars

back in their case. 'Quite keen. I find their behaviour fascinating.'

'I suppose it's a quiet, peaceful hobby,' she said dubiously, which he obviously translated into, 'At least it's something to do in the country,' for his tone grew sharp.

'The birds and animals are part of our life, as we are part of theirs.' He looked at her. 'Do you know anything about them?'

When she shook her head he looked very disapproving. 'Everybody should know something of the world around them.' He opened his car door. 'Well, time I was off. See you sometime.'

He waved goodbye as he drove off. It was a pity he wasn't going in the other direction, Marla thought, because then he could have given her a lift back. As it was, the sun was setting and there was a cold wind blowing before she got back to the comfort of the stove and the armchair in her kitchen.

She wondered when she would see him again, and one late morning at work, just as she was starting to feel hungry, she was pleasantly surprised to see him appear in her doorway.

'I was just passing,' he explained smoothly, 'and I decided you might like this.'

'This' was something in a brown paper bag. It proved to be a large book whose cover showed a young boy gazing up at a tree, and was entitled *The Boy's Book of the Countryside*. 'I had it when I was a child,' he explained, 'and I decided you might be able to use it now.'

A quick look showed colourful pictures of plants, butterflies and birds, obviously suitable for someone with little or no knowledge of the subject. She had to admit to herself that that did describe her.

'Thank you,' she said politely. 'I suppose it could be useful.'

'Good. Well, it's one o'clock. Can I buy you lunch?'

Marla clicked on her computer to shut it down and picked up her handbag.

'I'll be delighted to have lunch with you,' she said, 'but on the understanding that I'll buy my own.'

'Certainly not. I've invited you, so I'll pay.'

They went to a pleasant, unassuming Chinese restaurant, and over the meal got to know more about each other's lives.

'Was it always taken for granted that you would be a solicitor?' she enquired.

John shook his head. 'My father was very careful to leave the choice up to me. I think he secretly hoped that I would turn out to be daring and adventurous, but I like the law — I like helping people and showing them how to be in control of their lives, and now he's approaching retirement I think he's glad I made the choice.'

'Well, I suppose it was very convenient for you to follow in his footsteps.'

She realised too late how patronising this sounded, and saw his lips tighten at the implications that he had taken the easy way in his choice of career.

'What about you?' he asked.

Marla laughed. 'My mother married young and never had a job — helping my father do up houses was her career — but I think she would have loved a more glamorous life, and as soon as I started appearing in school plays she assumed that I was going to be an actress. I think she really made the decision for me and was more disappointed than I was when I didn't do very well on stage.'

John's mouth twisted. 'It does sound as though you were fulfilling your mother's dream. Were you happy to do that or did you ever have your own ambitions to do something else?'

Ouch! He had certainly got his own back. 'Life as an actress and a model isn't the glamorous life that I thought it was going to be, but I have enjoyed it, and I didn't have any other burning ambitions. Anyway, I think Mother has given up hope of me being famous for anything. She and Dad are thoroughly enjoying life in Spain, and now she's just waiting for me to marry and start producing grandchildren.'

John looked at her thoughtfully. 'And is there any chance of that happening soon? Are you particularly interested in anyone?' He looked down. 'I'm sorry. I shouldn't have asked you that.'

'Why not? And the answer is 'no'. I've been too busy finding enough work to survive to have time for any serious romance.'

'Well, you've got a quieter life now, so perhaps romance is possible.'

The silence that followed was broken by Marla. 'I suppose it's possible,' she said. 'Have you got a girlfriend?'

He shook his head. 'Not at the moment. Of course I've had girlfriends in the past, but until now I haven't met one I wanted to spend the rest of my life with. I hope I do soon. I don't think I would feel my life was complete without a wife and family.'

'Your parents were very interested in Seth Yates' possible romantic life.'

He laughed. 'I told you we were rivals. They don't want him beating me to the altar.'

There was a pause, and Marla looked at her watch and took a sharp breath.

'Oh, dear, I've got to get back or Miss Charter will be very annoyed. She insists on punctuality. Thank you for asking me out. It's been a pleasant lunch. Now, let me pay my share.'

He shook his head. 'Certainly not.'

She said goodbye and walked away, only to hear him call after her. He was holding out her handbag. 'You've left this again.'

She stretched out her hand to take the bag, but he retained his grip on it. 'On the whole, I've enjoyed this lunch. We must do it again, and next time I'll let you pay your share.' Then he gave her the bag and walked away without waiting for her to agree. Arrogant!

It was a quiet afternoon and she found herself thinking about their lunchtime discussion and about Seth Yates. She had noticed that since his visit to London Seth's attitude towards her had changed. Previously she had suspected that he was often trying to flirt with her, but now his behaviour was that purely of a friend and neighbour. He no longer stood close to her, touched her hand when he gave her a parcel of eggs, or gazed into her eyes when he spoke. He must have realised that he was getting nowhere with her and given up.

At home she looked through John's book and decided that she had seen some of the plants and birds pictured. She got into the habit of going for walks after work in the surrounding country-side when the weather was good enough, and not only enjoyed the exercise but found herself noticing the wildlife and the various plants struggling to survive through the winter and afterwards. She looked for them in the book, always feeling very satisfied if she found and identified something. Returning from one walk, she saw herself reflected in a window. The rubber boots and old jeans were topped with one of Uncle Andrew's thick woollen jumpers. People who knew her as an elegant model would not have recognised her, but at least she was warm and dry.

6

She took John Ericson's remark about further lunches for mere politeness, but he did appear a couple of weeks later at lunchtime, and the week after that. At first she slightly resented his assumption that she would be free and willing to lunch with him whenever he felt like it, but found she enjoyed his unexpected appearances more than she would a regular engagement, a definite commitment. She liked the stimulus of his company, the occasional crisp exchange of near-insults. The arrogance and over-confidence which he had displayed in their early meetings faded. Perhaps it had been a defence mechanism. After all, people would have more trust in a solicitor who seemed completely sure of himself.

Then one lunch went on a little longer than usual and she realised that she was going to be really late back at the office.

'I've got to go!' she exclaimed. 'I've told you how Miss Charter insists on punctuality.'

John Ericson smiled lazily. 'It's all right,' he said comfortably. 'You just have to tell her you were with me and that it was my fault.'

'I don't think she will take that as an adequate excuse.'

He sighed. 'Marla, my mother and her female friends have decided it's time I settled down with someone, and apparently they all think that you would be a possible candidate. Miss Charter won't be too upset when she finds you were late because you were with me.'

Marla gaped at him and shook her head, trying to clear her thoughts. 'Don't tell me you see me as your girlfriend!' Her eyes widened. 'Do you?'

He laughed. 'No, but the fact that we see each other from time to time keeps my mother and her friends happy.' He gave her a sideways look. 'And who knows? Given time we might warm to each other.'

She stared at him, and then realised he was shaking with silent laughter. Relieved, she began to laugh as well. 'Let's just keep your mother happy with the occasional lunch, shall we? And now I really must go.'

Life at Fernwood House continued to have its drawbacks. She grew tired of having to light the fire if she wanted heat and hot water, and detested the dirty job of clearing out the ashes. She did not want to spend every evening sitting in an armchair and staring at the small television she had bought. One weekend she decided it was time to start using the sitting room, but when she lit a fire there the room rapidly filled with smoke, and even when she had opened the windows and managed to get a small fire going she found the room damp and depressing. Christmas was coming and she hated the thought of spending it by herself in that uncomfortable house. Sometimes, bored, she looked through the cardboard boxes stored upstairs, trying to find some clue to the missing years of Uncle Andrew's life, but her search was always unsuccessful and she began to suspect that he must have deliberately destroyed any trace of his past.

Then came a day which she would remember for a long time. It had been difficult at work. Everybody seemed bad-tempered and demanding, and Ted Barker had thrown a particularly nasty scene. Then her ride home was through heavy, cold rain driven into her face by a strong wind that threatened to blow her bike over. She was glad to reach Fernwood House and opened the door eagerly, hoping that now she would get cheered up a little. She picked up the post from the doormat and leafed through it eagerly, only to find it was all circulars. She stood in the kitchen, tearing off her wet jacket, and there were tears in her eyes. It was her birthday, and not one person had sent her a card! Of course, she was sure her parents would have remembered and the post from Spain could be a little erratic, so their card would probably arrive the next morning, but that was little consolation now. Didn't Sasha know her birthday, or was she too busy enjoying life in the West End to remember her friend? Wasn't there anyone who had thought of her?

She made herself supper and ate it staring out the window at the dismal rainy evening. When she'd finished the lonely meal, on impulse she lit one of the candles she kept handy in case of power-cuts, fixed it to a plate, and stood it on the table.

'Happy birthday to me!' she sang quietly. 'Happy birthday to me!'

She blew the candle out. That was the end of her celebrations.

Just as she was nerving herself to go and have a bath in the freezing cold bathroom, her phone rang. She was tempted to ignore it. It would either be Sasha, reminding her of the glamour of the stage and the pleasures of London,

172

or her father to wish her a happy birthday. He would take great pleasure in informing her that it was warm and sunny in Spain. But the phone continued to ring. Whoever was calling was determined to get in touch with her and it might be an emergency. Reluctantly she picked it up.

At first she did not recognise the high-pitched female voice.

'Marla? Is that you? Where on earth are you?'

Marla blinked, then her eyes widened. 'Felicity! Is that really you?'

'Of course it is,' said the voice, slightly aggrieved. Felicity Graham was an agent who had found Marla several modelling jobs in the past. 'It's taken me ages to trace you,' she was complaining. 'Finally I remembered that you usually kept in touch with Sasha Smith, so I contacted her and she said that you were living in the darkest depths of the country, hundreds of miles from London. Why didn't you leave your telephone number with my secretary?'

Marla allowed a slightly acid note to creep into her voice. 'After the incident at the motor show I got the impression you didn't want to hear from me ever again.'

'Oh, that was ages ago.'

'So why are you calling me now?'

Felicity's voice grew low and dramatic. 'Because I've got this marvellous opportunity for you. Lewis James, the designer, is putting on a special fashion show, and he has specifically asked for you as a model!'

Marla was too taken aback to speak. Lewis James was a young designer who was rapidly gaining increasing importance in the fashion world. Marla had modelled for a couple of his shows and the two of them had got on well at the time, but she had assumed he would have forgotten her by now.

Felicity's voice grew shrill and impatient. 'Did you hear me? Are you still there?'

Marla mumbled something incoherent and Felicity went on. 'Good. Now the show is in London in two weeks' time. You'll have to be here at least a week beforehand, of course.'

Marla interrupted her. 'But, Felicity, I can't do it! I've got a job here and I can't just abandon it for a few days' work in London.'

After a few seconds of stunned silence, Felicity exploded, 'Don't talk nonsense! This is Lewis James asking for you. You don't turn him down because of some dreary little job in some God-forsaken backwoods town. Do well, and you will get other jobs here.'

'It's too big a risk.'

'At least think about it,' Felicity wheedled. 'Oh, someone's calling on my other phone. I'll call you tomorrow and I trust you'll have come to your senses.'

The call ended. Marla put down the phone and sat back deep in thought. Felicity was right. This was a completely unexpected chance to escape from the monotonous dull life in this run-down house, to get back to the glamour of London. Her father wouldn't mind if she abandoned the house to the gentle care of the estate agent. But it was taking a big gamble. If the assignment did not lead to other work, then she would not be able to come back to Woodham. She would be homeless and jobless once again. She brooded on the problem as the fire grew low without being able to make up her mind. Then a noise disturbed her. Theo came into the kitchen, something dangling from his mouth. He trotted over to Marla and proudly dropped a dead mouse at her feet. She jumped up, screaming. The cat, upset by her reaction to his present, reacted by snarling and digging his claws into her leg. Marla fled upstairs where she slammed the bedroom door behind her and threw herself on the bed. That settled it! She would go to London!

It should have been very straight-forward the next morning. All she had to do was tell Miss Charter that she would be leaving. That would be that.

Goodbye to Ted Barker and his belligerent appearances, goodbye to all those niggling little problems she was expected to solve. Unfortunately, Miss Charter did not see it that way.

When Marla had nerved herself to knock timidly on Miss Charter's office door, taken a deep breath when she was called in and nervously announced her resignation, Miss Charter flatly refused to accept it.

'You can't go! You're needed here. You're doing a good job.'

'Thank you, Miss Charter, but you can't stop me and I am leaving.'

'Why?'

Marla told her, and Miss Charter turned crimson. 'You're leaving your job just to appear in a fashion show?'

'I'm leaving my job, I'm leaving the house, and I'm leaving Woodham. I was only supposed to come here for a few days. Somehow I've managed to get stuck here for months. Now I'm going back to the life I led before Uncle Andrew died.'

Miss Charter leant back in her chair and her normal colour returned. 'Let's get this straight,' she said firmly. 'You're being asked to appear in a fashion show, and it will take about two weeks.'

'And will probably lead to more work!'

'But it might not.' Miss Charter placed her hands flat on her desk and leant forward. 'I will not accept your resignation.' She held up a hand to silence Marla's angry protests. 'Instead I am giving you two weeks' leave of absence — unpaid. If you do get more fashion work, then you can let me know. If not, you can come back here where you are doing a good and worthwhile job. Now be sensible and accept my offer.'

Marla was tempted to refuse, to cut all links with Woodham ruthlessly as soon as possible, but she knew it would be foolish to do so. She had never been a star of the fashion world and her recent absence would mean that many people would have forgotten her as other would-be models clamoured for their attention. Reluctantly she agreed, infuriated again by Miss Charter's smug smile. Obviously the woman did not think that anyone else in fashion would want to employ Marla. Well, she would prove her wrong!

Marla had not expected to see John Ericson that day, but she was delighted when he appeared and whisked her off to lunch. She was keen to explain her plans to him, sure that he would sympathise with her eagerness to return to modelling in London, but when she told him her news he looked at her with horror.

'Leave Woodham? Go back to London for one show? What are you going to do if it doesn't work out?'

'I hope it will work out, but if it doesn't then, as I said, Miss Charter has given me two weeks' leave.'

'Suppose you get some follow-up work that takes you beyond the two weeks, and then nothing else? What then?'

Marla felt herself reddening with anger.

'I thought you'd congratulate me on getting the chance to do what I really want to do. Instead you seem to be taking it for granted that it's not going to work out the way I hope.'

John was shaking his head. 'Marla, you know I wish you well and want you to be happy, but face facts. You have told me about your attempts to build a career in acting or modelling, and they haven't been very successful, have they? Why should this be any different?'

'Lewis James has asked for me. He wants me for his show.'

'He wants you for a few days.' John hesitated. 'Look, you've told me about the modelling world, how there are thousands of girls every year all sure they are going to be top models. Don't you think that if you were going to be a success, it would have happened by now?'

She stared at him, momentarily silenced, and then found her voice again. 'Are you telling me that I am too old?'

'Not too old if you were already established,' he said hastily, 'but . . . '

Marla leant forward, interrupting him. 'I am being given a chance to do what I want to do, to return to London and a glamorous career, instead of being stuck here in this insignificant little town and spending my life dealing with its miserable inhabitants and their petty complaints. Unlike you, I have dreams.'

'But don't you see that that is all they are, just dreams?'

'I'm going to make them come true. I'm not like you. I'm not going to take the easy way and follow in someone else's footsteps. I'm going to fight to make my dreams come true!' Her voice had risen and she was suddenly aware that people at the surrounding tables had stopped their own conversations and were listening to her denouncement of their town. She pushed back her chair and stood up, abandoning her meal.

'I am going to London and I won't see you again,' she said coldly. 'Goodbye.' She seized her handbag and stalked out of the restaurant, back to her office, where she sat at her desk, suddenly overcome with remorse. She had publicly humiliated a young man she liked who had been kind and helpful to her since her first minutes in Woodham. From time to time she looked eagerly at the door, hoping that he would follow her so that she could apologise, but he did not appear. Obviously he would never want to speak to her again. It was yet another reason not to come back to Woodham.

The next thing was to tell Seth Yates. Cycling back at the end of the day, she knocked on Home Farm's door. He greeted her and asked her in. Standing in the warm, homely kitchen, she told him what she intended to do and waited defensively for his reaction. He had listened silently, his face showing no reaction to her news.

'So you don't think you'll be coming back here,' he said when she had finished.

'I doubt it. After all, I never meant to

stay here as long as I have.'

He nodded. 'What about the house?'

'I'm leaving that to the estate agent, though there doesn't seem any chance of it selling soon.' A thought struck her. 'There is one thing you can do for me. Will you look after Theo?'

For the first time he smiled. 'If he comes round looking for food I'll feed him, don't worry. When are you actually leaving?'

'On Saturday — two days' time. I'm going by train.' She had originally planned to leave a few days later, but now she wanted to get away as soon as possible.

Seth raised an imaginary glass to toast her. 'Well, good luck. Would you like a lift to the station on Saturday?'

She hadn't thought of this and accepted his offer gratefully before returning to Fernwood House. The fire was out, a cold wind was rattling the rotten window-frames, and she had run out of fresh milk. She sipped her black coffee as she looked around and decided she was doing the right thing. Woodham and its inhabitants would soon be forgotten when she reached London, and this time she was going to do well. Lewis James wanted her, and after his show so would other designers.

She rang Felicity Graham and said that she would take part in the fashion show. It was clear that Felicity had taken it for granted that she would.

Marla needed somewhere to stay in London but that problem was quickly solved. As soon as she had called Sasha with her good news Sasha insisted that she should stay with her.

'It would be marvellous if I could be with you, at least till I know if I will be staying in London or not,' Marla said, 'but have you really got room?'

'I haven't got a spare bedroom, I'm afraid, but I've got a very comfortable sofa-bed in the living room.'

'Then I'd love to come. It will be like old times.'

Sasha gave her a giggle. 'Not quite. I think we're both doing a bit better now.'

Her voice became more serious. 'What about the friends you've made in Woodham — your neighbour, Seth Yates, for example, and the young solicitor? How have they reacted? Won't you miss them?'

'They think I'm mad, but I don't care. I want to get back to London!'

'And I want to see you here!'

It did not take Marla long to pack her two suitcases. She was unpleasantly surprised by how tight her best suit was when she put it on. Sitting in an office, sandwich lunches and late-night snacks obviously had added a few pounds to her figure, but a week or so rushing round London should get rid of them, she told herself. While she waited for Seth early on Saturday morning she stood in the middle of the kitchen floor after checking that she had not forgotten anything. It was cold because she had let the fire go out so that she could clear away the ashes, and she found herself shivering. The house was cleaner and tidier than when she arrived, but that was all the difference she had made. She had left a full bowl of food by Theo's basket and now, moved by a sudden impulse, she bent down and ruffled his coat.

'Goodbye, Theo. Will you miss me?'

He yawned, fidgeted, and went back to sleep and she laughed.

'Well, at least I won't miss the dead mice!'

When Seth knocked on the door she opened it quickly and picked up her cases. She climbed into his vehicle and as they drove away she took one look back at Fernwood House as it stood once again cold and empty, slowly rotting away. She felt a pang of guilt which she quickly suppressed. She was a town girl and she was going back to her natural habitat.

There was a light haze over the fields. 'It's going to be a fine day,' Seth commented. 'Have you noticed how bare the trees are now? Soon, with a little luck, the fields will be covered with white snow glittering in the sunshine — and yet you're going to spend two whole weeks in dirty old London.'

'There are parks and gardens.'

He waved a hand at the fields. 'Nothing like this. I've been to London a few times and I could never live there.'

There were very few people waiting at the station and Seth stood silently by her side till the train arrived. He handed her the two suitcases, his face serious. 'No regrets? You can still change your mind.' She shook her head and finally he smiled. 'Then goodbye, Marla, and I hope you get what you want. When you see your friend Sasha, give her my regards.'

She thought of that moment when she had seen Sasha in his arms. Had it been part of his tuition, a rehearsal of Restoration romance, rather than a genuine embrace? Then he closed the door, she took her seat as the train drew out of the station, and soon Woodham was behind her, part of her past, and London lay ahead.

The city came as a shock after the

quiet of the Cheshire countryside. She had forgotten just how noisy it was, and hated her journey on a crowded Underground train, crushed between commuters who all seemed to want to tread on her feet. She was glad to reach Sasha's address, a large Victorian house divided into flats, to press the bell and almost collapse on the mat as her friend threw open the door and welcomed her.

'You need coffee!' Sasha announced. 'I've got some waiting, so hurry up.' She seized one case, leaving Marla to bring the other, and led the way to a door off the entrance hall.

'Come in and sit down,' Sasha urged her friend, and bustled away as Marla sank down on a sofa. She could hear the sounds of cups clinking as Sasha poured the coffee, and soon her friend was back with a tray.

'I'll have to leave you soon,' she apologised. 'I like to get to the theatre for the matinee with a little time to spare, and I'll stay there for the evening performance. Make yourself at home and I'll see you later this evening.'

When she had gone and Marla had had time to recover, she began to look around. The flat stretched the depth of the house and while the living room was not very large, it was warm and comfortable and the furniture and decorations were in good condition. There was a double bedroom and a small but well-equipped bathroom. Beyond the kitchen window she could see a garden.

Success had evidently not turned Sasha into a cook, for she had left a couple of tins for Marla to heat for her meals. Marla ate, dozed on the couch, and watched television. When Sasha returned in the late evening she found her peering out at the lawn and trees and giggled.

'It's different from those awful bed-sits we had to stay in, isn't it? We used to have to sleep, eat and cook in one room and share a bathroom with other people usually. Now I've got a kitchen, a bathroom and a separate bedroom all to myself.'

Marla wondered how much the flat cost, but Sasha was rattling on. 'The girl I've replaced was going to have this flat, and Mr Somers arranged that I should have it instead for practically nothing. It's lovely to be able to spend a bit of money on being comfortable and not have to save every penny because you don't know when you are going to work again.'

'So I take it you know what you are going to do after the play ends?'

'I actually have a choice, though I have narrowed it down. I thought you could help me make the final decision. Now, have some coffee and tell me about Woodham.'

'Oh, nothing much has changed and nothing much has happened. I told you I had dinner with the Ericsons, the solicitor's parents, and that was a pleasant evening. I've had lunch with John a few times since then.'

'I thought you liked him, although he did annoy you sometimes. So will you keep in touch with him?'

'No. We had a big public row the other day — he thought I was a fool to leave Woodham and a steady job. So I don't think we are friends any longer.'

'And Beryl Richards? I was pleased to see her and her friend the night they came to the play.'

'That evening was the highlight of her life so far! Whenever I see her I have to tell her if I've got any news of you. At least she'll miss our chats about you.'

There was a pause. Sasha fidgeted. 'Who else? Oh, that neighbour of yours — Seth — the one who helped me. How is he getting on?'

'Did I tell you that he has seen your performance as well? I think he was quite impressed. He asked me to give you his regards when he gave me a lift to the station this morning. In fact he's the only person in Woodham who thinks I might make a success in London. I met his mother, incidentally. She wants him to get married.'

'Oh! Has she anybody particular in mind? Was she hinting that you would make a suitable bride?'

'It's possible! He's good-looking, helpful, hard-working, but I don't want to settle down just yet.' She closed her eyes. In Woodham she would have been in bed by now, and there was silence for a while until she sat up briskly. 'Now, tell me more about you. What choices have you got?'

It turned out that Sasha had received several offers, but was only seriously considering a role in a romantic comedy film and a stage role as the leading lady with a famous actor as her partner in a gritty modern drama.

'Which do you prefer?' Marla asked.

'Well, the film role would be well paid and I would have world-wide exposure. And the attraction of filming is that you only have to give one good performance, it's recorded, the bad bits edited or re-recorded, and that's that. The play would be a lot more demanding. As you once pointed out, on stage I have to give a good performance night after night, it's a difficult part, and I'd have to be good not to be completely overshadowed by the leading man.'

'So you prefer the film?'

Sasha shook her head slowly. 'It's tempting, but it's lightweight, and will probably soon be forgotten. The stage role is a challenge, and I think I'd learn a lot from the cast — they're all really good.'

'But you'll earn less?'

'It will still be more than I've ever earned before.'

They discussed the pros and cons of the two offers for a while, and then it was time to talk about Marla's immediate future.

'Were you surprised to hear that Lewis James wanted you for his show?'

'I was surprised at first, but we did get on very well together when I worked for him before. Anyway, I suspect that he specified half-a-dozen models, not just me.'

'And afterwards?'

'If I make a good impression then other designers might ask for me.'

'You definitely don't want to go back to Woodham?'

'There's nothing for me there that I'll miss — except for Seth, of course.'

They fell quiet and then Sasha looked at her watch and jumped to her feet. 'It's time for sleep. We can talk some more tomorrow.'

The sofa was soon transformed into a comfortable bed and Marla cuddled down, but it was some time before she could sleep. She could hear the noise of traffic, the sound of footsteps and people talking in the street outside, so unlike the deep silence which nightly surrounded Fernwood House. She found herself thinking about Sasha. At first she had thought her changed by success, but now she acknowledged that though Sasha had gained in confidence, money and fame were not enough to really change her. Basically she was still the girl who wanted above all to be acknowledged as a good actress.

Marla woke with a start the next morning at her usual early hour, but had to wait for some time for Sasha to emerge, yawning.

'You should have woken me up,' she reproached Marla.

'I've got used to getting up early and spending a couple of hours by myself. At least I don't have to light the fire or feed Theo here, or deal with the dead animals he sometimes brings home!'

She was due at Lewis James' studio at ten o'clock and made up very carefully, though she dressed casually in jeans and a loose top. Sasha persuaded her that it was worth taking a taxi so that she would not get lost in the maze of London streets and as a result she arrived early. She hesitated outside the unobtrusive side door of his premises, took a deep breath, and then pressed the bell. She was thinking of Sasha, who had been given her chance of success and taken it. Now it was her turn. She mustn't fail!

The door was opened by a middle-aged woman who looked at her coldly. 'Yes?'

'I'm Marla Merton. I'm one of the models for the show.'

The woman peered over her spectacles at Marla as if doubting what she said, then checked a sheet of paper among several gripped in her hand. 'Oh yes, here you are — Marla Merton. Come in.' She stepped back. 'Go straight through. Lewis is talking to the scenic designers now.'

Marla walked along a bare uncarpeted passage to the door at its end. Beyond was a very large room, now a scene of apparent chaos. A stage projected from one wall and the rest of the floor was taken up with racks of clothes and large tables covered with papers and bolts of cloth. Marla could smell the familiar mixture of expensive perfume and fresh sweat. Small groups of people clustered here and there, some waving their arms energetically to emphasise a point they were making, some gossiping, some quietly drinking coffee. Marla saw Lewis James on the stage, deep in conversation with two men, and decided to wait till he had finished with them before she made her presence known. She looked round, located a coffee machine, and told herself that she urgently needed some caffeine. As she filled her cup a tall, slender, elegant girl eyed her with curiosity. 'Are you one of the designers?' she asked.

Marla shook her head. 'No. I'm one of the models. I'm Marla Merton.'

The girl's eyebrows rose. 'One of the models?'

Marla's chin rose defiantly. 'Yes. Don't I look like one?'

The girl looked her over slowly and critically before replying, 'Well, you are a little generously built for a model.'

Marla felt herself flushing hotly. 'Haven't you heard?' she returned. 'Skinny models are going out. Normal size is the fashion now.'

Before any more could be said the two were interrupted by Lewis James. 'Naomi . . .' he began to the other girl, then glanced at Marla and stopped. 'Marla!' he exclaimed, seizing her in a bear hug. 'I've been looking out for you.' Now he stood back and looked her up and down and a slow smile curved his lips. 'You look great, and just right for the show.'

'Your friend here wasn't so sure.'

He half-turned to the other girl and laughed. 'Naomi still hasn't quite grasped the difference between this show and the usual catwalk display.' His tone was patronising and Marla saw the other girl look down, biting her lip at the casual humiliation.

The designer's arm slipped round Marla's waist with easy familiarity. 'It's going to be halfway between a fashion show and a theatrical performance, and I wanted you because I knew you were both a model and an actress. Come over to this table and I'll explain.'

He swept her over to a table piled high with large sheets of paper piled on top of each other and began to expand on what was planned, occasionally grabbing a diagram or list to illustrate what he was saying. 'Basically, we're abandoning the idea of the catwalk with a few models parading up and down. As you can see, we've got a stage, and we're going to show various scenes, such as a girl meeting a boy for the first time, two sweethearts choosing an engagement ring, a couple out for a stroll in the park. No words — just music to echo the action. Of course they'll all be wearing my clothes, and of course we'll have a wedding scene at the end, because wedding dresses sell well.'

'What's my part?' Marla enquired.

'Two girls are each trying to attract the same man. Naomi will be the other girl, and we have a really good-looking model for the man. You'll like him.'

'And who wins him?'

Lewis laughed, tilted her chin up with one finger and gazed into her eyes. 'You do, of course! Now I'll have to hand you over to the wardrobe people.'

Marla was very carefully measured — not only the usual bust and waist, but length of arm and leg, and size of wrist and neck. The dresses would be made to fit perfectly. Then she was given an outline of the scene in which she would appear, and directed to go and discuss it with Naomi. They found a quiet corner and pulled two chairs up to a table. Marla began to put forward her ideas for the scene as they came to her, scribbling notes down as she did so. The other girl was cool and unresponsive at first, but she gradually grew more animated and did offer some useful suggestions to add interest to the scenario. After a while they went for more coffee and gossiped casually. Apparently this was Naomi's first major show and she desperately wanted to be a success.

'Don't we all?' Marla said sadly.

'But given the chance, I'm sure I can be a top model!'

Marla remembered her own early dreams and kept silent.

After about another hour, she sighed and laid down the sheets of paper on which she had recorded their ideas. 'I've had enough for now.'

'It's time for another break,' Naomi agreed. 'Shall we go and have another coffee?'

'I was thinking more of something to eat — lunch,' Marla told her.

Naomi shook her head firmly. 'I don't each lunch.'

Privately Marla thought that Naomi looked as if she didn't eat breakfast, tea or supper either. 'You can have just coffee, but I'll have a snack.'

Naomi looked at her and raised an eyebrow. 'Is that wise?'

'It's necessary,' Marla said tersely.

In the improvised canteen Marla selected a ham sandwich and a latte, while Naomi limited herself to a black unsweetened coffee, and they managed to find a table in a corner. Marla saw how the other girl was eyeing the ham sandwich, so she cut it into quarters and offered one quarter to Naomi.

'Go on, take it,' she urged, but Naomi shook her head and drew back as if she knew the sandwich had been poisoned.

'I daren't! If I eat that, I'll want more, and I'll end up stuffing myself full.'

'Would that be so dreadful?'

'I want to be a top model. That means staying very slim.'

Marla stirred her own coffee slowly. 'As I said before, there is a move to have models nearer the size of the customers who buy the clothes.'

'Well, I'll wait till that move spreads. So far nobody has told me that I'm too thin.'

Marla bit into her sandwich, chewed, and swallowed. 'I'm afraid I've got into the habit of eating more during the past few months,' she said.

'Really? Where have you been? I haven't seen you around the dress shows.'

Marla explained how her uncle's death had taken her to Cheshire. She described her life in the small town, the characters she had met, what it was like to wake up to the sound of Seth's cockerels crowing, and Theo's tendency to bring her presents of dead mice. As

202

she described her life near Woodham she was suddenly aware of a longing to be back there, to be able to cycle through the fields with the sun on her face instead of being confined in this windowless building.

She saw that Naomi was looking at her with horror. 'It sounds terrible!' the girl exclaimed. 'Dead animals, no culture, just desolation for miles around!'

'It's not that bad,' Marla protested.

'Then why have you left it and come back here?'

'Because I'm a model and Lewis offered me work, which may lead to more work.'

Naomi's eyebrows rose again, but all she said was, 'Then I wish you luck. Now, as you've finished that enormous sandwich, shall we get back to our scene?'

7

Marla fumbled for the key Sasha had given her to her flat, almost stumbled into the hallway, and sat down heavily in an armchair, eyes closing. She only stirred when Sasha, already back from the theatre, came into the room, and then she gazed blearily up at her friend.

'A tiring day?' Sasha guessed.

Marla nodded, struggling to sit upright. 'Intensive and long,' she agreed. 'I'd forgotten how every tiny detail is fretted over.'

'But did you enjoy it?' Sasha asked anxiously.

This time the nod was emphatic. 'It was wonderful. I'd also forgotten how exciting the atmosphere is when you are preparing for a show.'

Over a soup and sandwich supper Marla told Sasha about the day and the people she had met.

'Naomi doesn't sound very friendly. I should look out for her.'

'Oh, she's all right. She reminded me of when I first started as a model — desperately anxious to succeed.'

But Marla did not tell Sasha what had really worried her — that all that long day she had felt, deep down, that she was an outsider; that at no time had she felt that she still really belonged to the frenetic fashion world.

* * *

The male model for whom Naomi and Marla were to compete appeared the following morning, and lived up to all expectations. His darkly handsome face and spectacular body had featured in several advertising campaigns, and when he greeted Marla with a smile and an appraising look from his long-lashed eyes, she could feel her heart beating a little faster while his gaze was fixed on her.

'And I'm Naomi,' said a voice behind Marla, claiming his attention, and the model switched his regard to the blonde girl, who spent the rest of the day trying to make sure that it stayed there. However, she did not always succeed. Neither she nor the male model, unromantically called Fred, had had any acting experience, and as the three of them went through their scene together Marla found herself giving them basic tuition on how to act rather than just parade the clothes.

'It's fortunate we've got you to help us,' Fred told her. 'Isn't it, Naomi?'

'I suppose so,' the other girl said grumpily. Then she shook her head and managed a smile. 'You're right. We'd be pretty hopeless without you to guide us.'

Heartened, Marla redoubled her efforts to improve their performance. Between the three of them they managed to think up an amusing and stimulating scene, till Marla had to warn them not to add too much.

'Remember, basically it's still a fashion show, and we mustn't distract all the attention from the clothes.'

However, she was pleased by the praise they received from Lewis James and the other organisers when they went through their scene before them.

'You've done a good job, Marla,' Lewis James murmured to her afterwards. 'They'd never have managed anything like that without you.'

The show had been carefully planned and most of the preparations completed before the models had been summoned to prepare for the final version of their scenes and to have their clothes fitted, but it was still exhausting work — Lewis James was insisting on perfection in the presentation as well as in the clothes, and when the various parts of the show were finally being integrated there scarcely seemed time to grab a coffee or a bite to eat.

'You're losing weight,' a wardrobe mistress told Marla, busily pinning and tacking. 'I'll have to take the waist in.'

Marla grimaced at Naomi, who was waiting to have her dress checked. 'At this rate I'll be back to my modelling weight and you'll be able to eat lunch!'

'Well, it does help the dresses look their best.' Naomi, wearing a deceptively simple dress, twirled round. 'Do I look all right?' she said anxiously.

'The dress looks beautiful and so do you,' Marla said sincerely. Naomi had the gift of making anything she wore look good. In her designer dress she looked truly beautiful.

'Do you think Fred will think I look good?'

'Of course!' Marla said firmly, though privately she doubted whether Fred ever really noticed how anyone looked except himself. She had decided that he was extremely handsome, extremely vain and not very intelligent. Naomi, however, obviously still thought he was marvellous.

Marla and Naomi were now on friendly terms. Marla had decided that Naomi's initial antagonism had been due to the younger woman's uncertainty and her lack of confidence as she tried to make her way in the competitive world of modelling. Once she had realised how much she could learn from Marla her attitude had changed, and she now regarded Marla as a big sister.

Each evening Marla went back to Sasha's flat, ate a hasty meal, and gratefully fell asleep on the couch, except for one evening when she went to see Sasha at the theatre. There was no danger of her falling asleep then. It was a brilliant production with some outstanding actors. However, the rest of the experienced cast did not overshadow Sasha. At curtain fall the applause grew noticeably louder as she came forward and curtseyed to the audience.

Afterwards Marla tried to convey to Sasha how impressed she had been, but had a sneaky feeling that Sasha was beginning to realise herself just how much talent she possessed.

'I've enjoyed every minute of this production,' she said, 'but I've got to widen my experience.' She looked at Marla a little defiantly. 'I've decided to turn down the film offer and go for the stage play. It's less money, less exposure, but I think it will be better for me in the long run.'

Marla laughed. 'Could you have imagined a year ago that you would be given the chance to make a choice like that?'

Sasha shook her head. 'There are times when I still can't believe it. My life has altered so much.'

Surprisingly soon, the day of the fashion show drew near. All seemed to be going well, and the models-cum-actors were told they could have some time off the previous day.

'You're all doing brilliantly,' Lewis James told them. 'Have a rest and come in bright-eyed and full of energy.'

'What are you going to do with your free time?' Sasha had enquired when she heard this. 'Are you going to sleep all day?'

Marla shook her head. 'I've spent day

after day sealed off from the outside world, scarcely ever seeing a gleam of daylight. I'm going out to find some fresh air.'

Sasha shrugged. 'And where are you going to find that in London?'

'There are plenty of parks.'

'True. Well, I haven't got a matinee that day, so I'll come with you.'

For once they had a full, leisurely breakfast and then made their way to the royal parks. Marla noticed that some of the shops already had decorated Christmas trees in their windows.

'Not long now,' Sasha said, noticing her glances. 'The play finishes just a few days before Christmas.'

It was a bright, sunny day, and crowds of Londoners and tourists had also decided to enjoy the weather in the capital's open spaces before winter finally closed in.

Sasha took a deep breath as they walked under the trees. 'You were right to want to come here. It's marvellous to be able to enjoy all this open space, wander in the open air and look at the trees.'

Marla nodded, but secretly she was feeling deeply frustrated. In Woodham she had been free to roam the fields by herself, scarcely seeing a soul, watching the birds fly overhead, listening to their song, and occasionally disturbing a scampering rabbit. Here she had to share the green space with hundreds of others, and the only birds seemed to be pigeons scavenging for bread from left-over sandwiches tossed at them. Suddenly she was homesick for Woodham and the people she had met there. What was she doing sacrificing that for this noisy, polluted London setting? She told herself not to be stupid; that the urge to run away back to Cheshire was due to her nervousness about returning to the fashion world after a long break. She would be fine once the show started.

The omens were good. On the day the audience included many celebrities as well as notable figures from the fashion world. Lewis James was everywhere, checking details, urging the models to do their best. He greeted Marla with a kiss.

'I'm relying on you to see that those two novices don't let me down,' he murmured, glancing at Fred and Naomi, who were both looking decidedly nervous now the big day was here.

'They'll be fine,' she reassured him, while feeling she had enough to do playing her own part without being made responsible for the other two.

Then the show started. It went well. There were some minor hitches; nothing the audience noticed, though Marla saw Lewis shaking his head in despair at one point. She stood in the wings together with Naomi and Fred, waiting for their scene. Their music started playing and she took a step forward and so did Fred, but Naomi did not move. She stood frozen, her face a mask of terror. Fred looked back at her, wavered, and began to retreat. Lewis on the other side of the stage was staring at them in horror. The music played on. A few more seconds and the audience would begin to realise that something was wrong.

Marla seized Naomi's hand and pulled her forward.

'Come on! Time to show off our pretty dresses!' she hissed.

At first it seemed as if Naomi would not move. Then she took a step forward, moving like a robot, then another step. Fred followed her.

'Smile!' commanded Marla.

Obediently Naomi's mouth moved into the semblance of a smile. Then suddenly she was walking forward freely, her smile lighting up her face. Fred and Marla gave each other a look of deep relief as the lights focused on them and their scene began.

It went well, their mime provoking laughter from time to time. They finished and the spotlight left them. Suddenly drained, they went backstage and sank down. An assistant bustled up.

'That was great!' she enthused. 'Can I get you anything? Wine, a cold drink?'

'I want a ham sandwich,' Naomi said firmly. 'In fact I want a thick ham sandwich with lots of mustard.'

The assistant retreated, promising to see what she could do, and Naomi turned to Marla. 'You saved us,' she said simply. 'If it wasn't for you I would have ruined the show and my career.'

'You hesitated for a split second,' Marla responded, 'and it was understandable. This was your first really big show.'

'It will never happen again,' the other girl promised.

Later after the show — clearly a great success — had ended to tremendous applause, the participants began to disperse. Fred waved goodbye casually, and Marla doubted if she would ever see him again. Naomi kissed her gratefully and promised to keep in touch.

Marla began to pack her bag with the cosmetics and other bits and pieces which she had brought with her. The show was over, so what happened next? Would someone in the audience have been so impressed that they were willing to offer her work? The next few days would show.

Then she heard footsteps approaching and looked up to see Lewis James coming towards her. 'I hoped to catch you before you left,' he began. 'First, I wanted to thank you for coping with that girl's stage-fright. It was a nasty moment.' He paused. 'And also I wanted to offer you a job. One of my house models has just announced that she's pregnant and won't be able to work for some time. Would you be prepared to take her place till she can come back?'

Marla stared at him, temporarily struck dumb. This was what she had dreamed of, had hoped would result from this show! Several months' steady work in a famous fashion house should get her modelling career back on course.

Lewis James grinned at her a little smugly, fully aware of the importance of what he was offering. 'I can't go into all the details now, of course. Come round tomorrow and we'll discuss everything.'

He turned to go but Marla stretched out a trembling hand and caught him by the sleeve. He swung back, probably expecting Marla to try to express her gratitude and thanks. Instead she was shaking her head.

'Lewis, thank you very much . . . ' she began.

He patted her hand. 'I know how you feel. We'll talk tomorrow.'

'But I can't accept the offer!' Marla burst out.

He stared at her in disbelief. This was probably the only time a model had refused such an offer from him. 'What?' he exploded.

'I can't accept. I — I've got other plans.'

He gazed at her for a long second and then nodded slowly. 'I understand. You're hoping to go back to acting. Have you had an offer?' Marla stared at the floor and he shrugged. 'Well, good luck, and I hope you don't regret your decision.' He frowned. 'Now who can I ask?'

Marla thought quickly. 'What about Naomi? She was very nervous today, but it was her first big show. She has the feel for wearing clothes, and she'll be a great model if she's given the chance. If she's your house model, you can train her.'

Lewis James pursed his lips. Marla's refusal was already forgotten; he was thinking of his next show. 'Somebody was asking about her; said she looked great after the first few seconds. I'll think about it.' He hesitated. 'Are you quite sure you don't want to do it?'

She nodded, not trusting herself to speak, and he smiled cheerfully and was gone, leaving Marla suddenly shaking so much that she could barely stand. Had she just made the biggest mistake of her life? All she knew was that when Lewis James had made her the offer, suddenly she had felt a great tide of revulsion at the idea of months spent in workrooms being draped with fabric, standing while clothes were fitted on her, parading before crowded audiences, only to emerge at the end of a long day to find herself in the noisy, busy, airless city. She looked round and saw that Lewis James was talking to Naomi, and that the girl's face suddenly filled with sheer delight and she began nodding vigorously. Oh well, at least somebody was happy.

That night Sasha's quick footsteps clicked on the hall floor as she hurried in the door, eager to hear how the fashion show had gone, but she halted abruptly when she saw Marla huddled in her dressing gown on the couch, a handkerchief clutched in her hand and her eyes red from weeping.

'Go on, ask me,' Marla said wearily, lifting her head.

'How did it go?' Sasha asked obediently, clearly bracing herself for news of a disaster.

'It was brilliant. Everything went perfectly. And afterwards Lewis James offered me a job as a house model.'

Sasha sank into a chair as if all her bones had turned to jelly. 'That's marvellous!'

Marla did not respond and Sasha struggled to sit upright.

'Isn't it?' More silence. 'So what's the matter?'

Marla burst into tears, managing to say between sobs, 'I turned the job down.' She covered her face with her hands, rocking backwards and forwards in misery. 'I was offered the job I've dreamed about and I turned it down. I've been an utter fool!'

Now Sasha was on her feet again, hands on hips, almost glaring at her friend. 'You did what? Why?' Then she was beside her friend, taking her hand in her warm grasp. 'What was wrong? Come on, you know you can tell me.'

Marla made a noise that was half a sob, half a laugh. 'I can tell you, but I don't think you'll understand.'

'Call Lewis James in the morning and tell him you've changed your mind.'

'It's too late. He's already asked someone else.' She grimaced. 'Oh, Sasha, you know what it is like to have one burning ambition, and to be given the chance to fulfil that ambition. I'm not sure you can understand anyone rejecting that chance. I'm not absolutely sure why I've done it.'

'Try me. But wait till I've made us both a cup of coffee.'

When she came back carrying two mugs Marla was sitting up and had wiped the tears away. She took her mug with a grateful smile, Sasha sat down, and there was silence while they both sipped the comforting drinks. Then Sasha put her mug down.

'Come on. I'm waiting.'

Marla held her own drink close as if for comfort, and sat frowning while she tried to find the right words.

'All the time we've been getting ready for the show I've been putting my heart and soul into it, trying my hardest. But all the time, somewhere inside me, there has been this cold, distant feeling, making me feel that I didn't really belong there among the models, the dresses, the designers. The show itself was great and I knew I had contributed a little to its success. But then, when Lewis offered me that job, instead of being delighted all I could feel was panic. I suddenly realised that my ambition to succeed as a model was a dream I had cherished since my early teens, and that I should have realised some time ago that I had grown out of that dream, that I no longer wanted to be part of that world. Do you understand?'

Sasha shook her head. 'No. I can't understand giving up a dream, especially when you can make it come true, unless there was something you wanted more. Is there something — or someone — more important to you?'

Marla did not reply and they sat in silence until after some time Sasha stirred. 'What do you want to do instead?' she asked quietly.

Another half-sob, half-laugh. 'That's the silly thing. I don't know yet. I just know that if I had accepted Lewis's offer I would have been trapped in something that would have stopped me finding out what I really want to make of my life.'

Sasha sighed. 'I'll just have to accept that deep down you feel you've done the right thing. But how are you going to decide what to do now? You can stay here as long as you like,' she added hastily, but Marla shook her head.

'Thank you, but I'm going home.'

'Home?'

'To Woodham.'

'So now Woodham is home to you?' Sasha said keenly.

Marla seemed surprised herself. 'Where else could I call home? You know, all those hours in the workrooms and the studios, coming out into the noise and bustle of London, I kept wishing for the quiet open spaces, the green fields and the birdsong. I missed them.'

'And I suppose you missed certain people too?'

A pause. 'Yes, I did, more than I expected to.'

This time the silence lasted for minutes, both girls deep in thought, till Marla struggled to her feet.

'Well, I'd better have a wash and get some sleep. Tomorrow I've got to think of another plan for my life.' She picked up her coffee cup to take it back to the kitchen. 'At least I can cut down on coffee. I've been drinking gallons of it every day.' She hesitated at the door. 'Sasha, I know you must think I've made a thorough fool of myself, and I think you're probably right. But in fact when I turned Lewis's job down I suddenly felt relieved, happy — as if I had escaped. The feeling didn't last long, but it was there.'

Sasha managed a smile. 'Then you did the right thing. And don't worry about the alternative life plan. I suspect you've already got one, even if you haven't realised it yet.'

* * *

Both girls looked tired the next morning as if neither had enjoyed a good night's rest, but after a late breakfast Marla sat back, sighed, and announced her intention of packing and leaving that day.

'I told you, you don't have to go!' Sasha protested, but Marla shook her head.

'Miss Charter will be waiting to see if I go back, and if I do go quickly I will still have a job, and there's no point in just hanging round here.'

'I'll miss you,' Sasha said sadly.

'And I'll miss you. I'll think of you at Christmas, going to party after party, while I'm on my own trying to keep warm in that miserable house.'

'You won't be on your own,' Sasha said quickly. 'As soon as the play closes I'm coming down to stay with you. We'll spend the holidays together.'

'I can't ask you to do that! You must have made other plans.'

Sasha shrugged. 'I've had one or two invitations from members of the cast but I haven't accepted any, and anyway

225

I'd prefer to be with you.'

'Are you sure? I'd love to have you with me but you know I can't offer you as much as they can.'

Sasha nodded. 'I like them, but we two have been friends for a long time, and that's what is important.'

Marla was looking happier. 'Thank you. And now I've got a whole kitchen to myself we can cook a proper Christmas dinner.'

'Do you mean you've actually learnt to cook properly?'

Marla giggled. 'I've not got that far, but people always say that Christmas dinner is the easiest meal of the year. You just put everything in the oven, leave it for hours, and make sure that everybody has so much to drink that they don't notice if the turkey is burnt. Anyway, it will be better than appearing in panto and trying to find some cheap restaurant that's open for a quick meal on Christmas Day.'

'That is very true,' Sasha said, shuddering at some of the memories.

She insisted on coming to see Marla off on the train. 'We'll catch up on all the news when I see you at Christmas,' she promised, and stood waving as the train drew out of the station.

Marla sat down and watched as the view from the windows changed from rows of houses to scattered buildings and then to open fields. She remembered her last journey to Cheshire, when she had expected to spend only a few days or a couple of weeks in Woodham until she found work in the city. Now, although she had spent only a comparatively short time there, she did indeed feel that she was going home. Yet the house was still damp and decaying, the winter was drawing in, and the scenery would be lost behind rain and snow. As for the people she had met, who did she really want to see again? She had come to see John as a friend, but now he would probably ignore her existence if he heard of her return. Seth was a pleasant neighbour but nothing more, and the others she had met were no more than friendly acquaintances. She gulped. Again she doubted her decision. She should have accepted Lewis's offer and stayed in London. Instead she had thrown away her big chance! But it was too late now.

It was raining when the train drew into Woodham Station — a cold, miserable, steady rain with a hint of sleet. Marla picked up her suitcases and found herself sneaking a look round, hoping that by some miracle she would see John there, as he had been at the coach stop the last time, eager to sweep up her luggage and take her to her house. But the platform was empty except for her own solitary figure and she trudged out, head down against the rain, and made for the bus stop. After a twenty-minute wait, during which she was soaked to the skin, a bus arrived, she climbed on board, and was eventually deposited near Fernwood House. There were no lights in Home Farm, and as her cold fingers fumbled with the key Marla remembered that she had emptied the cupboards of perishable food before she left for London. Oh well, a cup of hot black instant coffee would be quite comforting.

The house was cold, but no longer had the damp and dusty smell she had encountered the first time she had opened that front door. Quickly she made her way to the kitchen and put the kettle on, and was grateful to find a tin of soup and some oat cakes in a cupboard. She was accustomed to lighting the fire now and soon logs were crackling in the hearth, warming the kitchen. Marla sat in the armchair, the woollen blanket round her shoulders, her hands clasping the warm cup. She looked round, luxuriating in the quiet peace. If she had a home, this was it, and she was happy to have come back. She thought of her Uncle Andrew. Had he also willingly given up a busy life in the city for this peace and tranquillity?

There was an inquisitive meow and Theo glided into the kitchen. When he saw Marla the sound changed to a deep purr and he came to rub himself against her legs. Marla bent down and stroked him and he arched his back.

'Well, at least you are pleased to see me back,' she told him.

Later she cuddled down clutching her hot-water bottle, sleepily glad to be back in a proper bed instead of the narrow confines of a couch.

She woke early the next morning as wintry sunshine struggled through the thin curtains and she lay still for a few minutes, trying to decide what she should do that day. She would have to go into Woodham and stock up with food, that was obvious; and if she had to go into town she might as well call in on Miss Charter and see if she still had a job. Life must go on and money must be earned.

She had forgotten to set her alarm clock and arrived at the council offices some ten minutes later than her usual starting time. She knocked on the door of Miss Charter's office, heard a muffled summons and went in. Miss Charter was at her desk, a telephone clutched to one ear while with her spare hand she leafed through a pile of paper. When she saw Marla her eyes widened and she dropped the paper and beckoned her desperately.

'Get me that green file from the top of the filing cabinet!' she hissed.

Marla found the file and put it in front of her and Miss Charter opened it, seized a form, nodded her thanks, and resumed her conversation on the telephone. Marla still stood there and Miss Charter looked up at her impatiently, waving a hand in dismissal.

'I'll see you later in your office,' she muttered, and went back to the telephone. Apparently Marla still had a job!

So much had happened to her since Marla had last been in her office that somehow she expected it to have changed completely, and was a little surprised to see it the same as ever except for a pile of letters and forms on her desk. She had to remind herself that she had only been away a couple of weeks. Sitting down, she started to go through the papers, sorting them into neat piles according to their urgency. This was interrupted by a noisy rap on the door, and then the familiar figure of Ted Barker erupted into her office.

He halted a little way from her, obviously disconcerted by the beaming smile with which she greeted him and by her words.

'Hallo, Mr Barker. I've quite missed you.'

'And I've missed you,' he retorted. 'I've been in this office three times in the past two weeks and there's been nobody here, just a notice telling me to ring somebody. That's no good. I want to speak to someone face-to-face.'

'And what do you want to say?'

'I want to complain that our heating isn't working properly. Here it is, winter time, and the radiators are barely warm. We're freezing at night!'

Marla sighed sympathetically. 'Oh, I know just what it's like. My house hasn't got central heating, unfortunately, so last night I was huddled up in bed with one of those old-fashioned pottery hot-water bottles. It was better than nothing, I suppose, but I was still very cold.' She picked up a pen. 'Now, give me the details and I'll pass them on to the appropriate department.'

This was done more quickly than usual, as she had given Ted Barker no excuse for his usual bitter speeches denouncing the council's inefficiency and reluctance to help. As he left she called after him, 'By the way, Merry Christmas, Mr Barker!'

He gave her a baffled parting glance.

8

Minutes later Miss Charter made her appearance.

'Well, Miss Merton, I don't know what happened in London, but I'm glad to see you back. I've been doing your job as well as my own while you were away.' She indicated the paperwork covering the desk. 'Any problems?'

Marla shook her head.

'Good. Then carry on.' At the door she turned round. 'Incidentally, the girl on maternity leave has decided she wants to stay at home with her baby, so it looks as if your job is permanent.'

And she was gone.

So Marla carried on, glad to find no insurmountable problems lurking in the papers. When the door opened again she held up a hand without raising her eyes from the form in front of her. 'Take a seat. I won't be a minute.'

When there was no reply she looked up. John Ericson was standing in the doorway, still grasping the handle, as though he was about to change his mind and walk out without speaking to her. 'Good morning,' he said evenly. 'Miss Charter told me you were back.' When she did not reply he released the handle and moved closer. Uncomfortably aware of their last meeting, she did not look up to meet his eyes.

'I'm sorry things didn't work out for you in London,' he said with an obvious effort. 'I may have thought you were doing the wrong thing, but the failure must still have hurt.'

Now Marla did look at him, her chin lifted defiantly. 'I did not fail,' she said clearly. 'I was offered a very good job in London, but I chose to turn it down.'

He looked at her, at first with evident disbelief, but then, as she looked him straight in the eyes, he nodded slowly. 'So you chose Woodham.'

'No, I rejected London.'

His mouth twisted. 'Well, at least

Miss Charter is glad to see you back.'
He walked towards the door and then
swung back, frowning blackly. 'We can't
leave it like this! Stop what you're doing
and we can talk over lunch.'

'I'm busy.'

He came back to her desk and took
the form she was unconsciously creas-
ing from her fingers and smoothed it
out on the desk. 'It's lunchtime. You
need to eat and we need to talk. Come
on.' He waited, unmoving, until finally
she nodded.

'Very well. But first I want to apologise. I was unforgivably rude to you last
time.'

'I did provoke you a little. Now hurry
up, I'm hungry.'

They walked in silence to the Chinese
restaurant where they usually ate, both
careful to leave a clear space between
them. The owner came to greet them.
'Welcome back!' he said happily. 'We
haven't seen you for some time. Now,
do you want your usual starters? Seaweed for the lady and soup for the

gentleman?' He showed them to a quiet table, and they took seats facing each other and ordered their food. John leant forward.

'Now explain.'

'The show went very well. I impressed Lewis James sufficiently for him to offer me a job as a house model. I turned it down.' She stopped speaking and stared at him obstinately until he shook his head impatiently.

'All right. Now tell me why.'

This was the difficult part, the part she still didn't fully understand herself, and her voice grew soft and hesitant. 'There was more than one reason. I've done enough modelling to know that it is hard work with very little glamour, and if I'd taken that job I would probably have stayed in modelling but not enjoyed it. In fact it would have bored me. And after two weeks in London I realised I didn't want to live in a big city anymore. So I came back because I can stay here — at least until the house is sold, though that doesn't look likely at the moment — and I can earn enough to live on here.'

'So the only reason you came back here is because you couldn't think of anything better? Or have you decided what you want to do with the rest of your life?'

Her shoulders drooped despondently. 'So far — no. I keep trying to think of something I'd be good at and that I'd enjoy, but I haven't really come up with much.'

He sat back as if her answer satisfied him. 'Well, it will be Christmas very soon, so if I were you I'd wait till the New Year before I made any decisive moves.' Their first course had arrived and he picked up his spoon with evident appetite.

'At least Sasha is coming down for Christmas, so I can talk things over with her,' Marla remarked as she forked up the crisp green seaweed.

'Sasha? The actress?' He groaned. 'I won't get any work out of Miss Richards then. What about Sasha's family?'

'Her parents were divorced when she was young. Now her mother is in America with her second husband and her father is somewhere in Africa with his third or fourth wife.'

By the time they had finished their meal she was glad to feel that their friendship had been largely mended. She was relieved. He was a pleasant, intelligent young man. She had regretted hurting him and she wanted to stay on good terms with him. Their quarrel had not been completely forgotten, however. As he said goodbye to her he gave a sudden wolfish grin.

'At least you may now have some idea why I decided I wanted a life here rather than in London, and you can stop thinking of me as the man who decided to be a big fish in a little pond rather than face the competition of the big city.' Then he walked rapidly away, leaving her to stare after him. His words showed that her accusation had wounded him more deeply than she had suspected by his manner this morning.

She tried to put aside personal thoughts and worked steadily for the rest of the day. Finally it was time to close the office and make for the super-market to stock up on food. There were Christmas lights in all of the shop win-dows and displays of mince tarts and crackers in the supermarket. She would soon have to buy things like that ready for Christmas with Sasha.

Wandering along the aisles, trying to decide what was absolutely essential, she suddenly heard her name. 'Marla! Miss Merton!' Someone was waving, trying to attract her attention, and Marla recognised Mrs Yates, Seth's mother. She was beaming.

'This is a surprise! Seth said you'd gone away. He said you might be thinking of never coming back, but I was sure you couldn't leave Woodham.' She lowered her voice. 'Does Seth know that you've returned yet?'

Marla shook her head. 'I only got back last night so I haven't seen him yet.'

'He will be very happy when he hears,' said Mrs Yates, her voice full of meaning. She looked at Marla's basket. 'I should put those eggs back,' she advised. 'Seth will have plenty for you. Well, I'd better get on shopping.'

When Marla saw Mrs Yates a couple of minutes later, her mobile phone was pressed to her ear. Presumably she was giving Seth the good news.

At the checkout Marla impulsively added some paper decorations to her shopping. Some would be put up at Fernwood House, and one or two could cheer up her office.

When Marla cycled home through the dark she saw lights on at Home Farm. She passed it and reached Fernwood House with relief, wheeling her bike up to the house. It had been a long day and she wanted a rest. Then she gave a little scream as something moved by the front door.

'It's only me,' said Seth. 'Mother said you would be back any time now. She told me to bring you some eggs immediately and I've got a chicken for you as well.'

'Come in,' said Marla, surprised by how pleased she was to see him. 'I need a cup of coffee so I'll make one for you as well.'

Seth expertly lit the fire while she made them both coffee.

'Are you surprised to see me?' she said challengingly.

'A little. What happened?'

'I had a great time and I was actually given the chance to stay in London, but I realised that I'd changed my mind about being a model, though I haven't decided what I want to do instead. Does that sound silly?'

He grinned and shook his head. 'No. I know what it's like to want something and then, just when you begin to think it's within reach, realise you don't want it after all.' He sipped his coffee and it was clear he was not going to explain what he meant.

'Well, at least I'll be here for Christmas,' Marla said. She looked at him from under her eyelashes. 'Sasha will be here as well. Her play finishes its run soon.' Was she imagining things, or had his hand tightened round his mug?

'That will be company for you,' he said neutrally as if the news meant nothing to him, and he left soon afterwards.

Marla was in bed, asleep, soon after nine o'clock.

⋆   ⋆   ⋆

It was surprising how quickly she settled back into the routine she had acquired in Woodham. Sometimes her life before she came to the little Cheshire town seemed unreal, just a prelude to the daily round of going to the office, doing what she could for council residents, coming back to Fernwood House and cooking a simple meal, and then falling into bed. She had to tell herself that in fact she would only stay in Woodham till the house was sold or she had decided what she really

243

wanted to do and she set about finding what that would be. She spent two whole evenings listing her interests, trying to decide what work her past experience would suit her for, and was rather dismayed at the shortness of the resulting list. All her life since she left school had been devoted to trying to succeed in modelling and acting, but few professions could make use of the ability to walk down a catwalk or put on stage make-up. She told herself not to give up. Something would come to her, and meanwhile she could continue to cycle to the little town and back. Anyway, as John Ericson had pointed out, there wasn't much point in job-seeking just before Christmas. Sasha would arrive soon and she intended to enjoy the holiday season, to take part in all the little rituals and festivities that she had missed out on for so long. Already her paper chains were up in her office and scented red candles burned beside a miniature cradle scene.

A telephone call had confirmed that

her parents were happy for her to stay at Fernwood House, though her parents did invite her to spend Christmas with them.

'You'd love it here, darling,' her mother said. 'Great food, good weather, lots of fun.'

'It sounds great, but I've told Sasha she can come here.'

'Why not bring her as well? There are some very cheap flights.'

It was very tempting, but then Marla thought how Miss Charter would react if she told her she was taking another break — this time to go to Spain — and decided against it. She did not want to risk losing her job before she had found another one.

Decorations began to appear in house windows as well as in shops — even the icecream vans were playing carols as they drove along — and the magazines were full of suggestions for traditional feasts.

One morning Miss Charter appeared with a clipboard. 'It's nothing to do with work,' she said by way of greeting. 'I've come to see what you're going to do for the town's Christmas Festival.'

'There's a festival?'

'Every year, and it's great fun. We have Father Christmas, of course, and all kinds of activities. It really brings members of the Woodham community together.'

'But I'm not really a member of the community.'

'Nonsense! You work here, you live here, and we do expect council workers to support it. Now, what can you do? Can you sing or dance?'

'Neither.'

'That's a pity. But you were an actress, weren't you?'

'Occasionally.'

Miss Charter's face brightened. 'Then you must know how to use make-up. I'll put you down to help with the face-painting for the children.'

This didn't sound too formidable a task so Marla agreed to take part. 'And what do you do, Miss Charter?' she asked pointedly.

'Me? Oh, I tell fortunes. Give me a pack of cards and I send everyone away happy.'

Marla did have other worries. In spite of her light-hearted comments to Sasha, one obstacle to Marla's plans for cooking a traditional Christmas dinner was that she hadn't got the slightest idea how to go about it. One Saturday afternoon she was desperately leafing through a cookery magazine whose cover showed a smiling, perfectly groomed blonde standing behind a table laden with every kind of Christmas food, when there was a polite cough behind her.

'Don't you think that kind of magazine gives you an inferiority complex?' said John Ericson. 'My mother says that Christmas lunch is just a normal roast dinner on a bigger scale.'

'Your mother presumably knows how to cook a roast dinner,' Marla said bitterly. 'I've never done one.'

'That is unfortunate.' He laughed at her dismal expression. 'Cheer up! Put that magazine down and let me treat you to a hot chocolate.'

They hurried through rain which was threatening to turn to sleet, until they found shelter in a café and ordered hot chocolate and cakes.

'I thought all mothers taught their daughters how to cook a roast dinner,' John commented idly.

'Not mine. My parents used to buy a run-down house and we'd live in it while they did it up, and then they'd sell that house and we'd move to another wreck. A lot of the time we didn't even have a working kitchen. My mother was very good at painting and decorating, but we lived on stacks of toast and fish and chips. Then, just when house prices were starting to rise, they bought a large decrepit Victorian house with a big garden, converted the house into four flats and sold most of the garden to a builder who put up two more houses. My parents realised they'd made enough money to fulfil their ambition to buy a small house in

Spain and live there in reasonable comfort, and they are very happy there. Of course, they eat out a lot.'

'Do you miss them? After all, you expect to spend Christmas with your family.'

But Marla was shaking her head. 'Ever since I started earning a living I've been working at Christmas. It's the one time of the year when practically any young actress with a little experience can find work in pantomime. Last year Sasha and I were together. She was the princess and I was her lady-in-waiting. We were so tired on Christmas Day that we had a couple of microwaved ready meals and slept the rest of the time.'

'Then surely Sasha won't be expecting too much this year.'

'I'd like to make this Christmas something to remember. This may be the last time we will spend together and I want it to be special. Sasha is obviously going to be very busy from now on and I don't know where I'll be or what I'll be

doing.' She blushed, realising how inde-
cisive she must sound, but John did not
seem to have noticed.

'Well, at least there seems to be a
good chance of a traditional white
Christmas,' he observed. 'The weather
forecast is for snow, so you may be
trapped in Fernwood House for days,
living on cold turkey. Have you got a
good stock of firewood?'

She nodded. 'Seth cut a couple of
trees down recently and gave me lots
of logs.'

'Very kind of him. Make sure you've
got plenty of candles and matches as
well.'

When their snack was finished they
left, parting as usual at the door to go
their separate ways.

'Merry Christmas!' Marla said.

'Merry Christmas — and may you
and Sasha eat well.'

The estate agent's office was a few
yards away and Marla decided she
might as well confirm that there was no
risk of the house being sold from under

her before Christmas.

The agent was visibly amused.

'You're quite safe, Miss Merton. Nobody has even shown the slightest interest in viewing Fernwood House, let alone buying it. Perhaps in spring — people always feel restless then.'

But the very next day there was a moment when she wondered if he was wrong, when there was a knock on the front door and she opened it and saw that the caller had stepped back after summoning her and was gazing up at the front of the house. He was a man in his fifties, she guessed, in a rather shabby black overcoat and straggly grey hair which badly needed cutting, but from the way he was surveying the buildings she guessed he might be a potential viewer.

'Can I help you?' she said politely.

The visitor stared at her till she repeated her question a little impatiently. 'I'm sorry,' he apologised, 'but have I got the right house? I'm looking for Mr Andrew Merton.'

Now it was her turn to stare. 'Mr Merton? He was my uncle — but he died a few months ago.'

The man gaped. 'Dead? But he can't be! I don't believe you. I want to see him! I must see him!' He was speaking urgently, agitatedly, and stepped forward as if about to force his way past her into the house.

'I'm afraid you're too late,' Marla said, hastily beginning to close the door in his face. 'If it is a business matter, I suggest you go to see his solicitors, Ericsons, in Woodham.'

But the man had turned on his heel and was walking away as fast as possible.

Marla felt frightened, and thought of phoning Seth, but what could he do to protect her? He could spend the night with her in Fernwood House, but that would cause even bigger problems! In the end she locked the front and back doors and checked every window was securely shut before she went to bed.

The next day she was surprised to

receive a telephone call at work from the estate agent. 'Forget what I said the other day,' he told her. 'Somebody wants to look at your house and he sounds keen. Says he likes the description and the quiet position. The only trouble is that this afternoon is the only time he can view it.'

'But I'm busy at work; I can't get away!'

There was a sigh. 'Will you let me show him round by myself? We have got a key, remember, just in case this kind of thing happened.'

'Couldn't he wait till after Christmas? I've got a friend coming for the holiday.'

Another heavy sigh. 'Miss Merton, this is the first person who has asked to see Fernwood House. Even if he likes it, even if he can pay cash and wants to move in as soon as possible, he couldn't finalise the sale before Christmas. Let me show him round.'

'Very well then.'

Marla put the phone down, but it was a few minutes before she could concentrate on the forms piled in front of her. If this was a buyer, then she could be homeless again in a few weeks, and would either have to find somewhere to rent in Woodham or get a job elsewhere. She had been wondering about going to stay with her parents or applying for a job as a travel rep. Travel companies might regard her as a suitable applicant if she could say she sometimes lived in Spain and had a smattering of the language.

She wondered who wanted to buy an old-fashioned, isolated, run-down, unattractive house. Would she live there if she had a choice? Probably not.

With Miss Charter's consent, she left work a bit early, hoping to get home while the agent and his client were still there, but the house was closed and empty, so she went in to the estate agent's the next morning before going to work.

The agent shook his head when he saw her. 'I'm sorry, Miss Merton. No good news, I'm afraid. I was quite hopeful at first. The gentleman seemed very interested and insisted on going through the whole house very carefully, examining every room, but at the end he just said we might hear from him.' He frowned. 'I think he was just one of those time-wasters who like looking round other people's houses. To tell the truth, he didn't look like a man who could afford to buy a house — a bit shabby.'

Marla felt a cold shiver run up her spine. 'In his fifties, an old black coat, rather long grey hair?'

'That's right! Do you know him?'

Marla explained the man's unexpected appearance at the house and the estate agent looked grim. 'I don't know who he is, and he gave me a telephone number that wasn't working when I tried to contact him first thing this morning. He's probably harmless, but I suggest you make sure your doors are locked securely when you are home by yourself.'

Marla assured him she would. At least Sasha would soon be there to keep her company.

Mid-afternoon Marla had a surprise visitor when John's mother, Mrs Ericson, appeared. 'I called to see Marianne — Miss Charter,' she said, 'and I've been meaning to contact you.'

Marla tried to digest the fact that the formidable Miss Charter was called Marianne, and waited to learn the purpose of Mrs Ericson's call. Her visitor seemed a little embarrassed.

'It's just that John was telling me that you were worried about cooking Christmas dinner for you and your friend,' she said hesitantly. 'I don't want you to feel insulted, but can I solve the problem by inviting both of you to join us at our house for the meal?'

Marla's instant reaction was gratitude and relief. She and Sasha would be certain of a good meal which she wouldn't have to cook!

'Insult me like that as much as you like,' she said warmly, then hesitated. 'But I don't want to intrude on your family dinner.'

Mrs Ericson shrugged. 'Don't worry

about that. We always have about a dozen people.' She looked smug. 'My mince pies are famous, and one man told me he'd come just for my roast potatoes! Now, the only problem is how you get to our house. John could pick you up, because there won't be many buses that day . . . '

'There's no need for that,' Marla told her. 'My friend has a car so we can provide our own transport.'

That problem solved, Mrs Ericson left, and five minutes later Miss Charter appeared. 'I gather we'll be at the Ericsons' together on Christmas Day,' she announced. 'Well, we can be sure of a first-class meal.' She settled down for a chat. 'They're a nice family. They had a rough patch a few years ago when Mr Ericson was ill, but everything seems to be all right now.'

'I've only met John's father once, but he seems healthy enough. What was wrong?'

'Cancer. He was very ill for a few months. John had just qualified and he had been offered a job with a very prestigious firm in London. It looked as if he was on the fast track to a great career so it seemed as though Mr Ericson would have to close his business. But John knew how much the business meant to his father and so he chose to keep the firm going rather than take the London job. Then it took a long time for Mr Ericson to recover and more time before he was actually fit enough to resume work. By then the offers had stopped coming in for John and he was committed to Woodham. He gave up a lot for his father. He seems happy enough, but he must be aware he has never fulfilled his potential.' She stood up. 'Well, I'll just go and make sure there haven't been any crises in the last few minutes. Then it's time for home.'

She went out, leaving Marla full of guilt as she remembered the time she had accused John Ericson of staying in Woodham because it was the safe, easy way.

Sasha had not been absolutely sure when she would be leaving London. There had to be an important meeting with her agent before she was free, but the following evening Marla was woken from a half-sleep in front of the television by the sound of a very noisy vehicle stopping in front of the house, followed by the triumphant honking of a horn. She opened the front door, and in the light that streamed out she saw Sasha waving at her from Esmeralda. Her friend got out and patted the little car proudly.

'She came all the way from London without any trouble! And I found this place again with only two wrong turnings!'

Marla threw her arms round her friend. 'Congratulations! I'm delighted to see both of you. Now come in and have a hot drink and tell me everything.'

Sasha was bubbling with news and couldn't wait to tell Marla. 'This morning I signed the contract to appear in the theatre early in the New Year. And

I'm getting paid twice what I was! Even when I got all those good reviews my salary wasn't increased by much.' She smiled teasingly. 'But guess what else I'm going to do?' She could not wait for Marla to guess. 'I'm going to Hollywood! The timetable for the film I told you about has been rearranged. When the play has finished I can go to America and make the film!' She was laughing. 'I only learnt this today, and I still find it difficult to believe.'

'It's going to be a big year for you,' Marla said. 'It's just as well we're having a quiet Christmas before everything starts.'

Sasha looked round and saw the miniscule Christmas tree in one corner and the bunch of holly by the door with two paper garlands stretched tightly across the ceiling. 'You're not going overboard with the decorations, are you? You should see Oxford Street.'

'I can imagine it,' Marla replied. 'But not so many people are going to see this place.'

'We'll have to make it more festive for Christmas Day and our big meal.' She grinned. 'I can't wait to see if you actually can cook a proper Christmas meal for us.'

'I'm very sorry, but you'll have to wait to find that out,' Marla retorted. 'We've been invited out for Christmas dinner by a woman who is supposed to be one of the best cooks in Cheshire.' She explained what had been arranged. 'So you will get a chance to meet some more of the people I've told you about.'

'You mean I'm going to meet Miss Charter?' There was a pause. 'So what are other people doing?' she asked, apparently casually.

'Who do you mean?' Marla asked, deliberately not understanding.

'Well, for example, Beryl Richards; and there's your neighbour — what's-his-name — the one who helped me.'

'Oh, you mean Seth. Presumably he'll be with his parents. He won't be at the Ericsons' anyway. He and John are not that fond of each other.' She was interested to see that Sasha looked a little despondent at this news.

In fact, Seth appeared the next day. He nodded coolly to Sasha but spoke to Marla. 'I've brought you some eggs, of course, but I've also brought you a chicken. However, don't think it's for your festive dinner. I am under instructions from my mother to ask you both to dinner on Christmas Day.'

Marla took his gifts gratefully, but shook her head.

'Thank your mother very much, but you're too late, I'm afraid. We've agreed to go to the Ericsons'.'

He did not show any strong reaction to this news. 'Mother will be disappointed. Oh well, I'll tell her you were already spoken for. Incidentally, have you got enough wood still?'

They chatted for a few minutes more and then he left. Sasha had not said a word.

Christmas was upon them. Like every other year, shops and advertisers had warned the public to be sure to get ready for the celebrations early but there always seemed to be plenty of time, until suddenly Christmas was only a few days away — days which seemed to pass very rapidly.

Marla was given an afternoon off and she and Sasha spent a happy time shopping in Woodham's main street. They had promised not to go over the top with presents for each other, but Marla found herself buying some expensive perfume for her friend and was sure that Sasha was guilty of equal extravagance. Between them they bought a special bottle of wine to give to the Ericsons.

They had driven into town in Esmeralda, but the little car was reluctant to start for the return journey, made some very peculiar noises on the way home, and stopped at Fernwood House with an apparent death-rattle and refused to show any sign of life when Sasha tried to start her again. She was distraught.

'What can I do? How will I get her back to London?'

'We'll phone a garage.'

'Most mechanics take one look at Esmeralda and refuse to touch her!'

'I'll ask people at work tomorrow if they know anyone who might help.'

In fact, to her surprise it was Miss Charter who had an idea.

'Why don't you ring Ted Barker?' she enquired when told of the problem.

'Ted Barker?'

'He's a very good mechanic, and he owes you some favours.'

'I haven't seen him for a while. I was beginning to wonder what was the matter.'

'Ring him. He can only say no.'

Nobody had a better idea, so Marla dialled the mobile phone number she had for Ted.

'Ted Barker!'

'Er — Mr Barker — this is Miss Merton from the council.'

'Yes?' A wary reply.

'My friend's car has broken down and Miss Charter said you might be able to help.'

There was a short silence, followed by a cautious, 'I might. What's the car?'

Marla gave Esmeralda's make and age, and waited for him to laugh and ring off. Instead he actually sounded interested.

'I haven't seen one of those for a long time. Where is it?'

She gave him her address and he said he'd be along 'sometime'. This did not sound too hopeful and she was therefore pleasantly surprised when she got home that evening to find a white van parked in the road while Ted had his head buried in Esmeralda's engine and Sasha was hovering nervously nearby.

'Hallo, Mr Barker,' Marla said loudly.

He lifted his head, looked at her, grunted, and plunged back into the bowels of Esmeralda. Occasionally he would hold out a hand and issue an order to Sasha, who would fumble in the toolbox on the ground and find the implement he wanted. Marla went indoors to change and make herself a cup of tea. When she went outside again the bonnet was shut and Ted Barker was talking earnestly to Sasha.

'I've got her going for now, but she won't last long.' He poked a finger at a rust patch and the metal seemed about to give way. 'Treat her carefully, but start looking for another car when you get back to London.' He put his tools away and rubbed his hands on a large handkerchief, obviously preparing to leave.

'How much do we owe you?' Marla asked, but he shook his head.

'Nothing. You've helped me in the past, so I'm repaying the favour.'

'Well, next time you come in to see me I'll make sure you get help extra quickly.'

He was still shaking his head. 'You won't be seeing me in your office again, Miss Merton.'

'Why? What's happened?'

He was looking smug. 'I've bought a house. It's a big old Victorian building that had been subdivided into three flats for years and it's been badly neglected, but I know I can turn it back into a great home. Of course the family will have to rough it for some time till it's sorted out. It's cold, and the plumbing doesn't always work, so we're really just camping in it at the moment, but it will be worth it in the end. I can do a lot of the work myself, and I'll be very careful who I choose to do the rest.'

Marla thought of all the times he had sworn his cherished family could not live in a house with a small leak or with heating that was not working at 100% efficiency. She also spared some pity for the tradesmen who would have to satisfy Ted Barker.

'I hope it all goes well,' she said warmly. 'You must come in sometime and tell me how it is going.'

He nodded, then reached into his van and brought out a small, gaily wrapped package which he gave to her. 'Just a little present to thank you for your help in the past. Merry Christmas!'

Without waiting any longer, he

swung himself into the driving seat, reversed, and drove away.

Inside the house, the girls found that the parcel held a box of chocolates, which they greedily opened.

'I'm glad Esmeralda is back in working order,' Marla observed. 'It's the Christmas Festival I told you about tomorrow. I have some stage make-up which we can use, and the local amateur dramatic society is supplying more in case a lot of children want their faces painted. I'm assuming you'll help me?'

'Of course! I'm expecting to meet Beryl Richards there, and her friend.'

9

Even early in the morning there was an air of excitement and anticipation in the centre of Woodham. Decorations crisscrossed high above the main street where market stalls were being set out with Christmas goodies, and carols could be heard from strategically sited loudspeakers.

Marla saw Miss Charter dressed in brightly coloured flowing robes and wearing a vivid headscarf. She waved airily at the two girls and promised to tell their fortunes if they had some spare time.

Marla and Sasha were shown to a little booth outside the council offices. It had a table and four chairs there already and Marla and Sasha soon laid out their collection of stage make-up. In a few minutes a woman appeared who greeted them like old friends. She dumped a large bag on the table. 'I've brought you all the make-up the drama society had.'

Sasha peered into the bag. 'We'll never use all this up!'

'You'll be surprised. The little darlings love going round all day looking like clowns.'

She was proved right. At first, about ten o'clock, a few children appeared clutching their parents' hands and demanding to be painted. Then more arrived, till by lunchtime there was a queue. Someone came to ask them if they would like to take a lunch break, but they looked up from the faces they were busy painting and shook their heads.

'We're too busy! Just bring us some sandwiches and a couple of coffees.'

Part of their appeal was because they asked the children what they wanted to look like instead of making them all look the same. This took a little longer, but there were some very satisfied princesses and some scary demons when they had finished. Some parents were sure their little darlings would refuse to have their faces washed come bedtime.

John Ericson came to say hello, wearing a waxed jacket over a rather garish knitted jumper. 'Don't say a word!' he warned Marla when he saw her eyeing it. 'An aunt knits me one every Christmas. I wear it once so I can truthfully tell her I have worn it, and then I put it away and forget about it.'

Beryl had obviously been telling everyone about Sasha, because more than once they caught the whisper, 'She's a proper actress, you know.' Sasha muttered that probably no one would have known if Beryl hadn't told them.

For her part Marla was surprised how many greeted her by name. She recognised council tenants she had helped, people she worked with, as well as shopkeepers. For a few hours she felt that she really belonged to the town.

When the festival finally ended with Father Christmas being driven away by real live reindeer, the two girls were happy but very tired.

'Well, we've done our bit for

Woodham,' said Sasha. 'Now we can relax for the rest of the holiday.'

Christmas Day and lunch at the Ericsons' was two days away. Marla's main problem was what to wear for the big day. In London Sasha had treated herself to a concoction in red and black with a big swirling skirt, but Marla had few formal clothes and those she had were too skimpy for mid-winter in Cheshire. On Christmas Eve she went through her wardrobe with her friend, but it didn't take long and at the end she decided sadly that she would have to settle for a skirt and blouse — respectable, but not impressive. Then Sasha had an idea.

'Hold on! What about all those clothes upstairs — the ones in the boxes?'

'They're decades old!'

'They're retro, just coming back into fashion. It's worth having a look, anyhow.'

They opened the boxes and began pulling out all the dresses. 'This is hopeless. There's nothing here,' grumbled

Marla, but Sasha had seen a glimpse of red and was now pulling out a bright scarlet dress. She held it up. It had a straight skirt and a bodice ornamented with two rows of brass buttons.

'Try it on,' Sasha commanded.

The soft wool flowed over Marla's body as she stepped into the dress, pulled it up and straightened it out, and then turned to Sasha.

'Perfect!'

Looking in her bedroom mirror, Marla had to agree. The design was so simple that it had not dated and the style suited her figure. Mentally she thanked the unknown woman whose clothes had been abandoned in this lonely house for some mysterious reason.

'If there are no more problems, we can relax for the evening,' Sasha said firmly, so they sat in the kitchen, warmed by the wood fire. Sasha and Marla shared a bottle of red wine and they talked over the day. It was a restful, contented scene. Theo, avoiding the bad weather outside, lay purring by the fire.

'It's Christmas Eve, after all,' said Marla. 'We should start celebrating. When my parents and I were together we would be hiding from each other, busy wrapping up the presents we had bought, then stealing into bedrooms later to put them by the bed. Of course we were always wide awake, but we pretended to be asleep.'

Then Marla shifted restlessly. Sasha looked at her enquiringly. 'I was just thinking,' said Marla, 'that this will be the last Christmas Eve we will spend together like this. Next year you will have had another triumph on stage and you'll have been to Hollywood and appeared in a film. You'll be world-famous! You'll be spending Christmas somewhere grand, surrounded by people eager to keep you happy by doing everything for you.'

Sasha considered this picture. 'It's possible,' she conceded, 'but it could still all go wrong. Anyway, I can always run away and find you. Where do you think you'll be?'

Marla shrugged. 'I don't know. I'm

still thinking about working in travel, or I could train for something. I suppose it's even possible that I could still be here.'

'Here's not so bad,' Sasha said comfortably. 'Remember what it was like that year when we were in panto in Blackpool? That was worse than last year. We got back to our bed-sit at midnight after the cast had a party, fell into bed and didn't wake up till late on Christmas Day. I think we had a tin of soup for our Christmas dinner, and we spent most of the day in bed because the room was so cold.'

This led to other memories of the past they had shared, until Marla looked at the clock and sighed. 'Time for bed. It's a full day tomorrow.'

Sasha stood up. 'It's been a good evening,' she said. 'Whatever happens in the future, we'll have our memories and we'll stay friends.'

The sky the next morning was heavy and dismal. Some scattered flakes of snow fell, then stopped, but there were few signs of a true white Christmas. Sasha received her present of perfume from Marla with obvious pleasure, and in return produced a cashmere scarf with a well-known designer's logo.

'I thought it might help to keep you warm in this desolate northern area,' she explained. 'Do you like it?'

'I love it!' Marla replied. 'But don't let any Cheshire people hear you running down their county.'

Just as they were finishing a late breakfast, Seth Yates knocked on the door.

'Not more eggs?' enquired Marla as she held her dressing gown tightly round her and told him to come in out of the cold.

'I just thought that as I won't be seeing you for lunch today I should come round and wish you both a merry Christmas.' Suddenly he whipped out a spray of mistletoe, held it over her head, and kissed her on the cheek. Then he turned to Sasha, who had stood up and begun clearing away the breakfast dishes.

'And, of course, a merry Christmas

to you as well,' Seth said, one hand seizing her shoulder as she tried to back away. He held the mistletoe up again, leant forward, and kissed her full on the lips. Then he released her instantly and laughed. 'Now I'll be able to tell my grandchildren I once kissed a famous actress,' he said, before turning and making for the front door.

Marla was laughing, but Sasha was scarlet with anger or embarrassment.

'Stupid idiot!' she muttered, but Marla shook her head.

'He's a young man with two attractive young women next door, and it's Christmas. We'll probably get kissed a lot more today.'

They took their time getting ready for lunch at the Ericsons', changing into their formal dresses and carefully applying make-up until they could sincerely congratulate each other on their appearance.

'Now let's hope Esmeralda starts,' Sasha said, taking out her keys. Esmeralda, however, was in a good mood after Ted

Barker's work and started without any trouble, and they reached the Ericsons' house at the appointed time.

Mrs Ericson opened the door and welcomed them in. 'Nearly everybody is here now,' she told them. 'Come into the living room to meet people and have a drink before the meal.'

As she had predicted, there were about a dozen people. Miss Charter was there, but Marla also saw Beryl Richards, who greeted Sasha with open arms and a squeal of pleasure and demanded to be told all the latest news about the London theatre scene. It was soon clear that the other guests had been made well aware that Sasha was a rising star, and before long she was the centre of a group, telling them about her hopes of Hollywood. Marla and John Ericson stood a little apart.

'I've got a feeling we're all going to remember that we once had Christmas dinner with Sasha Smith,' he observed.

Marla nodded. 'She's going right to the top,' she confirmed, and then, bracing herself, turned towards him. 'I owe you an apology,' she said formally.

He raised an eyebrow. 'Do you? For what? I thought you'd already said sorry once.'

'I apologise for being such a stupid, ignorant idiot. Miss Charter told me about your father and why you stayed in Woodham.'

His face froze for a second, and then he was frowning heavily. 'She shouldn't have told you. I don't want your pity!'

'You're not getting it. I just feel guilty because I jumped to the wrong conclusion. After all, why should I pity you? You've got a secure future, you're highly respected in the town, and you've got a family and home . . . ' She stopped, thinking to herself that she had none of those things.

The frown had changed to a slightly sardonic smile. 'The truth is,' John said deliberately, 'that I regretted the London opportunity for a short while — not because of the career opportunities but just because I wanted to prove to my peers what I could do. I knew I could have an outstanding career. But when I had to choose between that career and staying here for my father's sake it didn't take me long to decide. I know I am lucky to be here, and I am happy. So I accept your apology, and let's forget the matter and have another drink before Mother announces lunch.'

Lunch, which began twenty minutes later, was a formidable, delicious feast, full of delectable surprises as well as traditional fare. The long succession of courses was punctuated by jokes and laughter and the snap of crackers being pulled. Seated between John and a local bank manager, Marla enjoyed every minute. This was how she had always imagined Christmas should be; this was what Dickens had celebrated, and she was glad to be part of it.

Afterwards they all collapsed sleepily in the drawing-room and talked about the past year and what they expected to happen in the next. Once again Marla envied them their place in society, the fact that they felt secure in Woodham. Even Sasha could predict her future with some certainty. She, Marla, was the only one who seemed to have lost her way.

She was very aware of this when she was chatting to Miss Charter and the older woman asked if she had yet come to any decision about her future.

'If you did decide to stay here, we could send you on various courses, you know. You have ability. You might end up taking over my job when I retire.'

Marla smiled, unable to tell her that the idea of ending up as a spinster whose life was devoted to forms and regulations filled her with horror. She knew this was unfair, for by now she had realised that Miss Charter was very happy with her life, enjoying both her work and her circle of friends

Mrs Ericson, determined that no guest should go home hungry, produced Christmas cake and mince pies, and it was eight o'clock before the guests finally summoned up the energy to thank their hosts and start making their way home.

'We had a great time,' Marla assured her hostess. As she made her way to where Sasha was waiting with Esmeralda, she found John beside her.

'Now we've got things straightened out, perhaps we can make a fresh start,' he suggested quietly.

She looked at him. He could be annoying and awkward, but he had a lot of good things going for him. She smiled and nodded as he held the car door open for her.

'Then I'll see you soon,' he promised.

'What was that all about?' enquired Sasha, starting the car. She had limited herself to one glass of wine and a lot of orange juice.

'Just a misunderstanding we've cleared up.'

Sasha glanced at her. 'He is a very pleasant young man.'

'I suppose so, though I'm not sure that 'pleasant' is always the first word to come to mind.' She giggled. 'He hasn't got Seth's glamour, anyway. I wonder what lunch would have been like with his parents?'

'Would you have preferred that?' Sasha asked quickly.

'At least I wouldn't have been having lunch with my boss and my solicitor. That was a bit intimidating at first.'

'Of course. I'd been wondering how I would get on with Miss Charter. She did look very forbidding, but after a couple of drinks she was telling some rather rude jokes.'

'I didn't hear that! And what about Beryl Richards?'

'We're old friends now, and I've got some more autographs for her, though it's the gossip she really likes.'

It was not long before they were approaching Fernwood House. Home Farm was in darkness. Seth must still be celebrating with his parents. Sasha brought Esmeralda to a halt in front of the house.

'One more cup of coffee?' Marla enquired.

'Please. I'll just go and find my

slippers. These shoes are glamorous but they're killing me.'

Theo was prowling uneasily round the kitchen as she put the kettle on and spooned instant coffee into two mugs. It had been a good day, but she was ready for a restful hour before bed.

'Marla!'

It was a desperate whisper. Marla spun round and saw Sasha in the doorway but she was not alone. Behind her Marla could see the man in the shabby black coat who had demanded to see her uncle and then had asked the estate agent to show him round the house. Now he was holding Sasha in front of him. One arm pinned her arms to her sides and the other was holding a carving-knife to her neck. As Marla screamed, he released Sasha and gave her a sudden push. She stumbled over to Marla, but before they could move the man was in front of them, the threatening knife waving menacingly in front of their faces. His eyes were fixed on Marla, on her dress.

'Emma!' he said hoarsely. 'You've come back and you're wearing the dress I bought you for Christmas. I was longing to see you wearing it for me. Then I came home early from a business trip because I couldn't bear to be parted from you. I was looking forward to the way you would welcome me, and instead I found you dressed for a journey, all your belongings already packed and gone. Christmas Day, and you told me you were leaving me for Andrew Merton!'

His eyes were glittering and he looked utterly crazy.

'But you're making a mistake!' Marla said desperately. 'My name's not Emma . . .'

He bared his teeth. 'Do you think I'm so stupid I don't know my own wife?'

Marla tried to think of some response that would calm the madman, but as she breathed in something caught at her throat and she coughed. Something in the air was hindering her breathing. Smoke.

'Marla!' Sasha said hoarsely. 'He's set

fire to the bedroom.'

He heard her and laughed. 'Yes, I set fire to the house. I am going to destroy everything that Andrew Merton possessed, everything he cared for — including you, Emma. I thought I'd killed you years ago, but you've come back. This time I'll make sure.'

Now tendrils of smoke were visible, curling through the open door.

'You'll be killed as well if we stay here!' Marla said hoarsely.

'I know. I've nothing to live for. We'll die together. The fire will purify everything.'

There was a sudden noise outside — shouting. The front door crashed open, and John Ericson and Seth Yates were in the room.

'Fire! Get out at once!' John was yelling and then both young men saw the man and the knife, and came to an abrupt halt.

'What the hell is going on? Let them go!' John said urgently.

The intruder shook his head, smiling.

'Let them go, do you hear? The house is on fire and if you don't get out you'll be burnt alive!' The man nodded. 'Yes, that's right. I've told them we're all going to die.'

'Sasha has nothing to do with my uncle. Please let her go,' Marla begged.

The knife advanced, the point piercing her skin. 'Everybody dies!'

Now the fire could be heard crackling above them and the smoke was growing thicker.

While John and Seth watched helplessly, the man took a menacing step forward, the knife pressing even harder against Marla's throat, and she could feel a drop of blood oozing down her skin. But he had not seen Theo. The cat, agitated by the noise and the smoke, was stalking round the room, and as the man came closer to Marla his foot trod on Theo's tail. With a sudden yowl of protest the cat leapt up and sank his claws deep into the man's leg. He jerked back and cried out in surprise, and in that instant John had leapt forward. He hit the man so hard that he fell to the floor, the knife skittering away, and John seized Marla while Seth grabbed Sasha. The two girls found themselves half-carried, half-dragged out of the house to where John's car stood on the road. Marla clutched her rescuer, drawing in deep, unsteady breaths. Then she turned to look at the house. Now flames were clearly visible in the upper storey.

'Where is he?' demanded Seth, still holding Sasha.

'Still in the house,' responded John. 'Look!'

The would-be killer, instead of trying to escape, had retreated up the stairs. They saw him silhouetted at a bedroom window, the flames behind him, and Marla turned and buried her head on John's breast.

There was the sound of an alarm speeding through the lanes and they saw a fire-engine driving towards them at top speed. Seth shook his head savagely.

'They're too late. They won't save the house and they won't save him.'

It was clearly a hopeless task, but still the firemen rapidly set up their apparatus as John told the chief fire officer what had happened. His arm was still round Marla, and he turned to Seth, who was still clasping Sasha.

'We can't do anything more here. I'll take the girls home to my mother.'

'No!' Seth said sharply. 'Sasha stays with me. She's mine.'

Sasha said nothing, but held on to him even more tightly, and John shrugged.

'Very well. I'll contact you tomorrow. Marla, get in my car.' He released her but she was shaking, barely able to stand by herself, and he opened the car door, picked her up and put her on the back seat. Marla was barely aware of the journey, scarcely heard Mrs Ericson's exclamations, and was just conscious of drinking some hot milk before Mrs Ericson gently removed her dress and tucked her into bed. She stirred as the woman went to switch off the light.

'The house! That man! What has happened to him?'

'We'll find out tomorrow,' promised Mrs Ericson, and left Marla alone in the dark.

She woke the next morning with a dull headache and a vague feeling that something dreadful had taken place. As her memory of the scene at Fernwood House returned she tried to sit up, but sank back, feeling stiff and sore. A couple of minutes later the door opened and Mrs Ericson came in with a tray.

'I heard you moving so I've brought you coffee, fruit juice and cereal,' she announced. 'Eat what you feel like, and just tell me if you would prefer anything else.'

Marla ignored the food. 'Last night . . . ,' she began.

'Last night was a tragedy, but everything is under control now, so eat your breakfast while I run you a bath,' Mrs Ericson said firmly.

Obediently Marla drank some fruit juice, decided she could manage a cup of coffee, and then finished off the cereal. Next she stripped off the remainder of the previous day's clothes and sank gratefully into a deep, hot, scented bath, where she lay for some time while the stress gradually left her body. When she finally wandered back into the bedroom, wrapped in an enormous bath towel, she found basic underwear, a pair of jeans and a jumper waiting on the bed. She glanced in the mirror as she brushed her hair and decided that she looked almost normal apart from the deep bruise-like shadows under her eyes. The previous night Mrs Ericson had put a plaster on her neck where the knife had wounded her, but she took it off and found the mark was scarcely visible, already healing.

When she went downstairs she found Mrs Ericson in the kitchen, deftly removing the remaining meat from the carcass of the Christmas turkey. It seemed a very long time since it had appeared for the Christmas meal. Incredibly, it was less than twenty-four hours.

'Prepare yourself for a lot of cold turkey,' Mrs Ericson greeted her. 'Usually only the family have to suffer, but as a guest I shall expect you to eat some as well. Would you like another coffee?'

When Marla nodded she quickly filled a mug from a percolator — proper coffee, not instant, Marla noted.

'Those clothes don't look too bad,' observed Mrs Ericson. 'What do you want me to do with that red dress you were wearing? I can get it cleaned.'

Marla shuddered. 'No! I never want to see it again. Burn it!'

There was a quiet interval.

'Do you know what's happened?' she enquired after a few sips of coffee.

Mrs Ericson put down the knife. 'John has given me the general picture. He's over at Fernwood House now and he'll be able to fill in the details when he gets back.' Her face grew serious. 'First of all, that man — the one with the knife — was killed in the fire. As you know, the house was well alight

292

before the fire service could get there, and I'm afraid they couldn't save anything.'

'Sasha? My friend?'

Mrs Ericson smiled broadly.

'She's safe. I've had a call from Mrs Yates. The poor woman was completely bewildered when Seth arrived there last night with a girl who he said had been rescued from a madman and a fire, that she was a great actress and was, incidentally, the woman he loved. Did you know that?'

Marla was wide-eyed. 'I hadn't the slightest idea! I thought they didn't even like each other.'

'So we'd all like to hear the explanation.' Mrs Ericson looked at her watch. 'It's nearly lunchtime, so we'll have some turkey sandwiches, and later someone is going to bring Sasha over here.'

It was Seth's father who drove Sasha, and who disappeared instantly to talk to Mrs Ericson, tactfully leaving Sasha to throw her arms round her friend and dissolve into tears.

'Oh, Marla, I'm sorry, so sorry, but I couldn't do anything about it!'

'Of course you couldn't,' Marla told her. 'That man was out of his mind and threatening us with a knife.'

'Not that,' Sasha wailed. 'I mean Seth.'

'What about him?'

'I knew you cared for him, so I tried not to have anything to do with him, but yesterday, when he took me in his arms, I couldn't hide what I feel for him any longer.' She looked at Marla defiantly. 'We love each other.'

'Good.'

Sasha stared at her friend in bewilderment. 'You don't mind? You must mind!'

Marla shook her head, laughing. 'I don't know where you got the idea, Sasha, but I do not want Seth. He's an attractive man, and a very good neighbour, but he doesn't turn me on.'

'But every time he was mentioned you were saying how marvellous he was.'

'I like him very much. He's been a good friend, but that's all.'

Sasha seemed almost indignant. 'How could you stop yourself falling for him?'

'I managed it somehow, but apparently you couldn't.'

Sasha smiled, misty-eyed. 'The first time we looked at each other there seemed to be something joining us. Seth says he felt it too. But I didn't want to hurt you, so I avoided him.'

'I did see you kissing once.'

Sasha buried her face in her hands. 'We had been dancing together, close, our hands touching — but I had to pretend to be furious, tell him that he was never to touch me again, because I thought you wanted him and that he felt the same about you.'

Marla embraced her friend again. 'Well, I'm glad the two of you have finally sorted out how you really feel.' She frowned. 'The actress and the farmer. What happens now?'

A big sigh from Sasha. 'We don't know. We can't be together all the time because neither of us is willing to give up our way of life, our separate careers.

So we will be together as much as we can. I will always have time free throughout the year when I can come here, and Seth can come to London when I'm appearing there. His parents have agreed to look after the farm for a couple of weeks later in the year so he can join me in Hollywood. It will be difficult and it may not work out, but we'll try our best.'

'Seth in Hollywood! All those glamorous actresses will be fighting you for him!'

'Well they won't get him. He's mine!'

Soon afterwards Mr Yates took Sasha back to his home and Seth, and an hour later John finally appeared. He looked tired and there were smudges of dirt on his clothes.

'I've been to Fernwood House — or rather where Fernwood House used to be,' he said when he saw Marla looking at his dirty shoes. 'I'm afraid there's nothing left. It was a very intense fire and we suspect that Brian Soames used petrol in the bedrooms to get it started.'

'Brian Soames?'

'The man who held you at knife-point. His body has been recovered.'

'But who was he? Why did he want to destroy everything?'

John sat down in an armchair. 'I've spent a lot of the day trying to find that out and I can tell you that Boxing Day isn't the best time to try and get information. Apparently he was the business partner of your uncle, Andrew Merton. Soames had a beautiful wife called Emma. She and your uncle became lovers and she was getting ready to leave her husband when Soames came back unexpectedly early from a business trip and found her ready to leave him and go to Andrew Merton. They quarrelled, and she ended up at the foot of the stairs with her neck broken. Soames claimed it was an accident, and there was no way of proving it wasn't, but he went to prison for manslaughter. Your uncle was heartbroken and shut the business down before moving here. Soames had a mental breakdown in prison and when he came out he was living in a hostel under close supervision. Then a couple of weeks ago he vanished. Somehow he had found out where your uncle had moved to and was determined to hunt him down. You know the rest.'

'So my uncle lost his business and the woman he loved, and spent the rest of his life by himself in Fernwood House.'

'With the clothes which she had already packed up and sent to him.'

There was silence, and then Marla stirred. 'I have to thank you and Seth for saving our lives. How did you arrive at that moment?'

'Once again you had forgotten your handbag, and I was driving over to return it. When I got to Home Farm Seth was just dashing out of the gate. He had seen flames in your bedroom window as he drove up to his house, so after calling the fire brigade he was on his way to Fernwood House to see what he could do. When we saw that little green car and realised the two of you were in there we were horrified. Then we went in and found you with a knife at your throat! It was definitely a Christmas Day to remember.'

'God bless Theo,' Marla said with deep feeling.

'Yes, indeed. And he got out safely, by the way.'

At Mrs Ericson's insistence she spent the rest of the day quietly, but the following morning John agreed to her request to be taken to Fernwood House.

'Don't be upset,' he warned her, but nevertheless there were tears in her eyes when she saw the pile of blackened rubble.

'Everything's gone. Uncle Andrew's memories, those clothes, the things Sasha and I brought.' She groaned. 'I haven't anything to wear apart from what your mother has lent me!'

'At least the insurance payments were kept up,' John said practically. 'Our firm can lend you enough for things like clothes till the money comes through.' He looked up. 'Here comes Seth.'

The two men greeted each other warily, then John wandered off after a strong hint from Seth that he wanted a private word with Marla.

'I understand Sasha has told you about us,' he began.

'Yes. Congratulations! I'm sure you'll overcome any problems between you.'

Was there a hint of surprise at her sincerity? Had he also thought she might be falling for him? This was partly confirmed when he went on.

'You know, Marla, when you first came here I thought we might end up as a couple. After all, a beautiful model and a bachelor farmer become neighbours — it wouldn't be too unlikely.'

'And the idea appealed to you?'

He poked the toe of his boot into a pile of ashes, avoiding her eyes. 'Until I met Sasha. Then I knew that if I couldn't have her I didn't want anyone else, though marrying you would have had one big incentive. Fernwood House would have come back into my family's ownership — the family that owned the

300

manor here for centuries.' He looked at the pitiful ruin and shrugged. 'Now it's gone and I doubt if anyone will bother to rebuild it. I'm going to forget about the past. Sasha is my future.'

John was wandering back and Seth said goodbye to the other two. Back in the car, John looked at her inquisitively. 'Anything interesting from our farmer friend?'

'Not really.' She laughed. 'Apparently both he and Sasha thought I might end up with him.'

'So did half of Woodham,' he told her.

'What? Did you?'

'I wasn't sure.' He started the car while she thought about this. 'Is there anything else I can help you with?'

'Not today, but as soon as the shops and businesses reopen I'll have to start looking for somewhere to live.'

'You know you're welcome to stay with us as long as you like,' he said quietly.

'I know, and I'm grateful, but I should get my own place.'

'And you're going to look in Woodham,

not go back to London with Sasha?'

'I know it sounds silly, but losing the house has made me realise that I'm coming to regard this town as my home.'

He was smiling. 'And what will you do here?'

'Take up Miss Charter's suggestion of going on some courses.'

Unexpectedly he drew to a halt by the side of the road and turned to her. 'I told you why Miss Charter offered you your job in the first place.'

'You said it was something to do with your mother finding out that Miss Charter needed someone urgently. Fortunately she thought I could cope.'

'Marla, I told you once that my mother and her friends thought you would suit me. In fact, half of Woodham thought you would end up with Seth Yates. The other half thought you should end up with me. Well, I discovered from talking to my mother last night after you'd been tucked up safely in bed that you and I really have been the victims of a conspiracy.'

She jerked upright and stared at him. 'What do you mean by that?'

'After you had been to my office a couple of times Beryl Richards took it upon herself to tell my mother that she thought you were the perfect girl for me.' As she started to speak he held up a hand. 'Wait! There's more. It looked as though you might leave here at any moment, so after my mother had been told about you, she and her friend Miss Charter decided that if you were suitable you should be kept here by the offer of the office job provided you seemed capable. That tactic worked. And remember when I first took you out to lunch? Miss Charter had told me to give you some papers, remarking at the same time that it was nearly your lunchtime, so I had to take the hint.'

Marla fumbled with her seatbelt, ready to get out of the car and storm away. 'How ridiculous! Well, you can tell your mother and her friends that I do not feel obliged to fall in with their plans!'

'Do you have a choice?'

'Of course I do!'

'Marla, Christmas night you were a damsel in distress and I rescued you. You've heard enough fairy tales to know what that means. The damsel always ends up with the man who saves her from the villain.' She looked at him uncertainly. He was smiling, but his eyes were serious.

'Marla, I don't care what my mother or the rest of the population of Woodham think. From the moment I first saw you I knew you were special to me. As we got to know each other I grew more and more fond of you, but I thought you preferred Seth Yates and I told myself that really I only cared for you as a friend. But when I saw you with that madman holding a knife at your throat I knew that you were more important to me than anything else in the world, and I would have died to save you. I know I'm not particularly exciting, but I can offer you a home and a family, which I think you really want. I'm talking about marriage.' He looked away, ruffling his hair with his hand. 'Maybe too much is happening all at once, maybe I should have waited, but at least think about it.'

She gazed ahead. 'We'd argue.'

'And then we'd make up.'

'I can't cook.'

'That is a big problem, but I'm sure my mother could teach you.'

She turned to him indignantly, saw the laughter in his eyes, and began to pummel him. 'If you want me you'll have to get used to egg on toast!'

He took her in his arms. 'Caviar or egg on toast, it doesn't matter so long as I am with you.'

As he kissed her she was sure that somewhere she could hear Christmas bells ringing.

THE END

We do hope that you have enjoyed reading this large print book.

Did you know that all of our titles are available for purchase?

We publish a wide range of high quality large print books including:
Romances, Mysteries, Classics
General Fiction
Non Fiction and Westerns

Special interest titles available in large print are:
The Little Oxford Dictionary
Music Book, Song Book
Hymn Book, Service Book

Also available from us courtesy of Oxford University Press:
Young Readers' Dictionary
(large print edition)
Young Readers' Thesaurus
(large print edition)

For further information or a free brochure, please contact us at:
Ulverscroft Large Print Books Ltd.,
The Green, Bradgate Road, Anstey,
Leicester, LE7 7FU, England.
Tel: (00 44) 0116 236 4325
Fax: (00 44) 0116 234 0205

HOLIDAY ROMANCE

Patricia Keyson

Dee, a travel rep, flies to the south of Spain to work at the Paradiso hotel. On the journey, a chance encounter with the half-Spanish model Freddie leads to the two spending time together, and she suspects she may be falling for him. Then Dee is introduced to Freddie's uncle, Miguel, who is particularly charming towards her — despite having only recently been in a relationship with fellow rep Karen. But when Karen disappears in suspicious circumstances, Dee must decide which man she can trust . . .

THE SECRET OF THE SILVER LOCKET

Jill Barry

Orphan Grace Walker will come of age in 1925, having spent years as companion to the daughter of an aristocratic family. Grace believes her origins are humble, but as her birthday approaches, an encounter with young American professor Harry Gresham offers the chance of love and a new life. What could possibly prevent her from seizing happiness? A silver locket holds a vital clue, and a letter left by Grace's late mother reveals shocking news. Only Harry can piece the puzzle together . . .

THE AWAKENING HEART

Jean M. Long

When Tamsin's uncle and aunt take a holiday, leaving the family business — Lambourne Catering — in the charge of the younger generation, everyone must pitch in. Working at a near-disastrous dinner party, Tamsin meets Fraser, whose initially abrasive attitude hides a warm and understanding man beneath. Despite herself, Tamsin feels a growing attraction to him. But Rob, the man who broke her heart years ago, has returned — and seems to be carrying a torch for her once more . . .

THE SWALLOW HOUSE SUMMER

Margaret Mounsdon

When Issy Dillaine discovers she was adopted as a baby, she sets out to discover all she can about Amy Grant, her birth mother. She never dreamt her quest for the truth would lead her into a world of Z-list celebrities — as well as the arms of investigative journalist Ed Stanwood. But Ed's uncle Jonathan Jackson was the QC who had headed up the prosecution team working to convict her mother of fraud . . .

A FRENCH PIROUETTE

Jennifer Bohnet

After an accident in rehearsals, Suzette, a famous French ballerina, disappears to an auberge in Brittany to recuperate. Libby, a young English widow, is starting a new life running the auberge, purchased from her old friend Odette. The summer is full of ups and downs for all three — Suzette meets Pascal, Libby turns the head of local vet Lucas, and Odette is thrilled when her pregnant daughter returns to Brittany — as they come to terms with the changes in their lives.

THE FAMILY BY THE SHORE

June Davies

An air-mail letter and wallet of photographs from Hong Kong bring unexpected — and shocking — news for Laura Robbins and her younger brother and sister at Spryglass, the tall old family house facing the seashore on the wild Lancashire coast. Their seafaring father's startling revelation from overseas changes everything forever. As well as great happiness, the months ahead hold heartache, conflict and tragedy for the family by the shore — not least for Laura, loved by two men but uncertain of her own feelings or future . . .